THE CASE OF THE CURSED RING

KITTY GORING INVESTIGATES

BOOK THREE

ELLA STRIKE

DEAR READER,

London in the 1920s is a glamorous and exciting city, but danger and death are never too far behind.

Join Kitty Goring and her group of Bright Young Things in the adventure of a lifetime as they race to catch a killer who lurks amongst them.

Each book in this series is a cozy period mystery that features our plucky heroine and her scrappy little dog, Scottie, who are aided in their investigations by a group of eccentric and lovable characters.

This book was written in the UK and edited in UK English. Therefore, some spelling and grammar will be different from US English.

CHAPTER 1

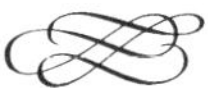

"Kitty, that dashed dog is at it again," snarled my brother Jimmy, bursting into the small parlour where I was curled up in the window seat with a book. "He's burrowing under my bed, and I simply won't have it! Call him off!"

"He's just doing his job, Jimmy," I said placidly as I turned a page in my book. "Scottie is in training."

"Training to dig all the way to China?" he scoffed.

"Don't be absurd, brother dear. I'm teaching Scottie to track and retrieve objects."

"But he's not a retriever, dash it," complained Jimmy. "You'd be better off training him to be a first-rate mouser."

"Scottie was meant for loftier things in life than hunting mice," I replied.

"Like what? Tearing up carpets?"

"Solving crimes! I wrapped a bone in a piece of cloth and buried it under a pile of old shirts under your bed for him to find. It took him a couple of hours, but I'm glad he's finally got the hang of it."

"But why did you do that? Now he won't rest until he's

laid waste to the rest of my room looking for more imaginary bones," wailed Jimmy.

"Oh, how you do go on, Jimmy! It is just one bone. And Scottie is smarter than you think. I'll have him trained to retrieve missing objects soon enough. You'll see," I said confidently.

"As long as you train him to leave my leather boots alone," grumbled Jimmy. "Training a terrier to be a retriever. What a ridiculous idea!"

"No, it's not! It's a brilliant one. And one that will make us a lot of money," I insisted. "I'm thinking of hiring my services out as a detective."

"A detective?" asked Jimmy in disbelief. "*You?*"

"Why not? I seem to be rather good at it. I solved the mystery of our missing silver. And I helped the police catch Jane's killer, didn't I? Not to mention the whole thing with Princess Noor's necklace."

"Yes, but Mother will never approve," said Jimmy glumly.

I sighed heavily. He was right. Our mother would have one of her spasms at the very idea of her daughter hunting missing objects at an age when she should be hunting a husband. Well, I'd just have to hide it from her, I decided firmly.

I had finally found my calling at the ripe age of twenty-three, and I wasn't giving it up to settle into boring domesticity. Scottie and I were going to make a fortune and a name. If only I could find a way to keep it from my mother.

"Speaking of Mother, here she is," said Jimmy. "And she doesn't look happy."

Mother staggered into the room with a letter in one hand and the other clutching her heart.

I jumped up to help her into a chair.

"Henrietta, Mother needs her salts," I called.

My mother's secretary, Henrietta Alton, hurried into the

room with a bottle of smelling salts and held it under Mother's nose.

"Are you ill, Mother?" I asked worriedly.

She groaned loudly and waved it away.

"Oh, take it away! It won't help me. Nothing will help me anymore," she wailed, looking alarmingly pale.

"What is the matter, Mother?" I asked, laying a cushion under her head. "Should I call for the doctor?"

In response, my mother pulled the cushion out from under her head and flung it across the room.

"Oh, what good is a doctor when you're saddled with an undutiful daughter? This is all your fault, Kitty!" she cried angrily.

I tried to remember what I could have done that was so dreadful, but I could think of nothing. I had been most dutiful of late, giving my mother no cause for complaint.

"Is this about the incident with the mouse, Mother? I assure you, Romley has aired the room thoroughly, and you can't smell the dead mouse at all."

Scottie had brought a dead mouse into the house and buried it in the bedroom next to my mother's. It took us three days to find out the source of the smell and three more days to get rid of it.

"This isn't about your beastly dog," cried Mother, and when Scottie let out a disapproving bark at her words, she shot him a fierce glare. He wilted under her glare, and she turned it on me next.

"Lady Belling writes to inform us that Benjamin has fallen in love," she announced.

"Well, he did drop in last week to tell us all about it. Did you forget, Mother?

"But I assumed that was one of his passing fancies. You know he falls in love at least once a week."

"If it has lasted so long, it must be serious," I replied. "I, for one, am very happy for him. Besides, it has nothing to do with us, Mother."

"And whose fault is that?" demanded my mother, sitting up. "You had every chance to secure his affections, Kitty. Yet, you let him slip through your fingers."

Benjamin Algernon Althorpe, the Earl of Belling, known to his friends as Bingo Belling, was one of our oldest friends. He was also one of the richest peers in the country, with vast estates in the south of England, which was the cause of my mother's current misery. Mother had always dreamed of having a rich son-in-law.

"I'm sorry, Mother," I said meekly.

It wouldn't do to argue with her when she was in such a state, but I couldn't quite picture myself married to a man with the intellect of a doorknob. Bingo, bless him, was gifted with the sweetest disposition - a necessary virtue, really, as his foolish antics could try the patience of a saint.

"I don't see why you're so upset, Mother. Bingo is always falling in love. And it never lasts," scoffed Jimmy.

"Lady Belling writes that it is very serious. He's... he's engaged to be married. Oh, I cannot bear it," she cried.

Bingo's love affairs never lasted more than a week, so if the latest one had resulted in an official engagement, it must be serious, indeed. When he was here last week, he did tell us that his lady love had accepted his marriage proposal, but I wasn't sure he could convince his mother to consent to the engagement. Apparently, he had convinced her, and I couldn't have been happier for my friend.

"That's wonderful news," I replied cheerfully.

"No, it isn't! Letitia says the girl is an opera singer," whispered my mother.

Jimmy let out a low whistle.

"Poor Bingo. His mother will never let him sully the Belling bloodline with an opera singer," he predicted.

"Letitia says he is being most defiant. He insisted on having his grandmother's engagement ring, and when she refused to hand it over, he said he'd buy the girl a whole jewellery store."

"Good for Bingo," I said approvingly.

It was high time he stood up to his overbearing mother.

"I hope this girl makes him happy," said Jimmy.

"Although I don't envy her having Lady Belling for a mother-in-law," I said

Lady Letitia Belling was a snob if ever there was one. According to her, no girl in the world was good enough for their family. I pitied Bingo's new fiancée, for Lady Belling was not the type to give up without a good fight. She would do her best to drive the girl out of Bingo's life.

But it seemed as if Bingo's love had prevailed, and his mother was forced to back down from her opposition to the marriage. There followed an official announcement in all the leading newspapers, and a week later, we received a gilded invitation to a grand party to celebrate their engagement.

The Dowager Countess of Belling
Cordially Invites You to Celebrate the Engagement of Her Son
Lord Benjamin Algernon Althorpe
The Earl of Belling
To
Miss Maria Bocelli
Join us for an evening of champagne, music, and merriment in honour of their union.
Date: Saturday, the 12th of September 1923
Time: Eight O'clock in the Evening
Venue: Belling House

"You know I can't abide ghastly new ballroom at Belling

House, Kitty. All that gilt and all those chandeliers will give me a headache," said Mother with a disapproving sniff. "I don't know what inspired Benjamin to have the room redone to resemble a flapper's boudoir. I have a good mind not to attend."

"Mother! Lady Belling is one of your dearest friends! She needs you to support her in this difficult moment," I said craftily.

My mother brightened at the prospect of a good gossip with the Countess of Belling over champagne and canapés and agreed to attend the party.

"All right, my dear. I suppose it *is* my duty to be by Letitia's side," she said with a martyr-like air that was belied by the gleam in her eyes. "Besides, it will give me a chance to wear my new gown."

I wrinkled my nose as I stared at her doubtfully. Her new gown was a ghastly chartreuse that was as expensive as it was awful.

"Surely not, Mother!" I said before I could stop myself.

My mother looked very offended at my exclamation.

"Whyever not?" she demanded.

"Well, I'm just worried you might blend into the gilt walls," I said tactfully.

"In that case, I'll have to make do with my old puce gown," she said, relenting, and I heaved a sigh of relief.

I didn't know what had come over her lately, but ever since we came into money again, my mother had lost her grip on taste and common sense. That is, if she'd had any at all.

"And I will wear my new emerald and gold striped coat with the red brocade waistcoat and my new purple cravat," said Jimmy, and I groaned loudly.

"You will look like a Christmas tree, Jimmy," I scolded, and he rolled his eyes in reply.

My brother had unfortunately inherited my mother's sense of style, and ever since he sold some of our lands to a developer at great profit, he seemed to be on a quest to indulge all his extravagant tastes. I would be very happy for him if only his taste didn't run to gaudy coats and ugly cravats. Not to mention the impossibly bright waistcoats he believed to be the height of fashion.

Jimmy defended his taste in clothes as vigorously as I abused it, and we were well on our way to having a rousing argument when Romley cleared his throat meaningfully.

"Lord Belling," he intoned, and Bingo burst into the room in his usual fashion.

"I say!" he cried, bowing hastily to my mother before he threw himself into the wingback chair opposite Jimmy. "I say!"

"What *do* you say, Jimmy?" I teased. "And is it too soon to offer my congratulations on your upcoming nuptials?"

"Thank you," he said, blotting his brow with a silk handkerchief. "But this is not the time for congratulations. I need help. I'm done for, Kitty."

I sat upright immediately.

"What's the matter, old fellow?" asked Jimmy lazily. "The Mater still giving you a hard time?"

"You don't know the half of it," replied Bingo fervently. "Have you seen the blasted thing?"

"What do you mean, Benjamin?" demanded Mother impatiently.

"The caricature, Lady Goring," cried Bingo. "*My* caricature!"

"Have you commissioned a caricature artist for your engagement party?" asked Jimmy. "How... droll."

"Don't be ridiculous, man! I'm talking about my caricature in a new scandal sheet that was delivered to our door this morning," replied Bingo.

"Heavens," gasped my mother, reaching for the bell immediately. "Romley, has a new scandal sheet been delivered to us today?"

"Not that I know of, your ladyship."

"Whyever not?" she demanded. "Oh, do go and check again, Romley!"

"It's a thin supplement. And rather tacky-looking," said Bingo, curling his upper lip in disdain. "The sort of sheet you'd throw away immediately without even reading."

"You really *are* a silly goose, Bingo," I said fondly. "If we came upon a tawdry scandal sheet, I assure you our first impulse will be to read it cover to cover, not throw it away!"

"I think I know the supplement that his lordship is referring to, your ladyship," said Romley. "From its green and orange exterior, I believed it to be an advertisement for a patent nerve tonic. I will fetch it at once."

"That's the one," cried Bingo, when Romley returned with a thin supplement on a salver. "Absolutely vile bit of trash."

"Yes, yes, my dear. Now, hush while I see what it has to say about you. Kitty dear, if you would just hand me my spectacles," said Mother, grabbing the sheet off the salver before we could reach it.

When she began to read, she let out a quick laugh before she pursed her lips and tried to keep a straight face.

"That is a great likeness of your dear mama, Bingo," she murmured.

"What does it say, Mother?" asked Jimmy impatiently.

"I'll tell you what it says," replied Bingo, instead. "It says the vilest things about my family! It claims that my mother and I had a big row over my grandmother's engagement ring!"

"But you did have a row about the ring," I pointed out.

"Well… yes! But they didn't have to print it in a rag! How

did they even know anything about it? It's as if the writer was in the room with us," he said furiously.

"It must be someone we know," said Jimmy.

I gasped in delight.

"What fun! Do you know what this means, Jimmy? It means we have an anonymous writer amongst us!"

"There isn't anything fun about it, Kitty," said Mother severely. "It is disgraceful. You do realise that none of us will be safe if there's a tattletale amongst us. Someone who reports our goings-on to the public."

"Come now, Mother. It is just a little harmless gossip," I said, rolling my eyes at her disapproving face.

"It ain't harmless, though," grumbled Bingo. "Look what it says about me! It calls me an earl with a spine made of sponge!"

"That *is* a bit rude," I said diplomatically. The trouble was it was true, even if it was rude. Bingo was one of the most spineless men I knew, which was why his mother got away with bullying him so mercilessly.

"And it makes Maria sound like a gold digger!" he went on angrily. "She is *not* a gold digger. She's an angel."

Jimmy and I looked at each other awkwardly while Mother let out a loud harrumph. We didn't have the heart to tell poor Bingo that his fiancée was most likely a gold digger, even if she claimed to love him dearly.

"I wonder if the writer will be present at your engagement party, Bingo," I said, trying to change the subject.

"I say! I hope not!" he cried in dismay.

"This bears investigating," said my mother, with a militant look in her eyes. "We cannot allow this writer to spy on us so shamelessly. I will be watching very keenly, Bingo. And if I spot anybody who looks as if they are writing this sort of rubbish, I will tell them off at once."

I had alarming visions of my mother accosting people at random and accusing them of writing this scandal sheet.

"How will you know whom to suspect, Mother?" I asked carefully.

She raised her chin and gave a disapproving sniff before she cast the sheet aside.

"Never you mind, Kitty dear. You're not the only detective in this family. I have some skills, too. And I'll prove it to you. I will find this sleazy writer before the evening is out. Just you wait," she said grimly.

I didn't know how the engagement party was going to turn out. All I knew was that between Bingo's fiancée, his mother *and* mine, we were in for an extremely entertaining evening.

CHAPTER 2

On Saturday, I stared at myself in the mirror as my maid, Florence, styled my hair in soft, glossy finger waves parted to the side and slid a slim, beaded headband into place. The tiny peacock feather on it was my only nod to the flamboyant fashion of the day. I smiled in satisfaction at my Lanvin chiffon frock in midnight blue with delicate beadwork across the bodice and a slim velvet ribbon to cinch the waist. It gleamed enough just to catch the light of the chandeliers without being gaudy.

Florence held up two necklaces, and I chose the long string of pearls, looping it around my neck twice.

"I'll wear the silver heels, Florence," I said, as I pulled on a pair of dove grey silk opera-length gloves. "And the pewter clutch, please."

When I was ready, I spritzed myself with my new favourite scent by Guerlain and grinned as Florence grimaced at the smell.

"It's too old for you, miss," she grumbled.

"I think, at twenty-four, I'm past the age of wearing

girlish scents, Florence," I said lightly as I slid my feet into my heels.

But it wasn't just my age. I felt I had matured suddenly in the past year. Dealing with the aftermath of a friend's murder and then getting entangled in a gruesome robbery and murder a few months later, had forced me to grow up in ways I hadn't expected. Soon after the war, I had chafed at the dullness of our lives in peacetime, turning my nose up at entertainments such as parties and balls because they were nothing to the excitement of the war effort. But now, I had learned to take joy in the little things because life was so uncertain. I was grateful for the privilege I had. The privilege of simply being alive and around my loved ones.

Mother looked resplendent in her puce silk gown and turban with the large, emerald green ostrich feather that bobbed over her forehead as she walked. She wore an emerald and diamond choker and a matching bracelet on her wrist.

"Where is the happy couple?" she cooed at Lady Belling, who was waiting to greet us as we entered the ballroom.

"Benjamin was right here," she said, looking to her right.

But Bingo was not where she expected him to be, and she craned her neck to spot him. When she did, she almost turned purple with rage because he was gazing lovingly into the eyes of a very flamboyantly dressed woman, who I assumed was his fiancée, Maria Bocelli.

"*Benjamin!* Come here at once," Lady Belling called out stridently.

Poor Bingo apologised to Maria and slunk back to his mother.

"Benjamin, I told you I must have you by my side to greet our guests," she said through gritted teeth.

"And I told you, Mother, that my place is with my fiancée. This party is in Maria's honour. I can hardly greet the guests on my own," he protested. "But you won't allow her to greet the guests at her own party."

"I refuse to stand next to that woman," snapped his mother dramatically. "If she's so eager to take my place, she will have to wait until I die. And I refuse to die early just to oblige that hussy."

Jimmy and I exchanged wide-eyed glances while our mother leaned forward to make sure she didn't miss a word of their argument. I had never seen Lady Belling so furious that she forgot herself completely.

Bingo looked like a cornered dog. He cast an embarrassed glance at Jimmy and me, almost as if he was begging us to rescue him. But Lady Belling was on the warpath, and there was simply no interrupting her tirade.

"Do something, Mother," I hissed. "This argument is extremely unbecoming. It should be reserved for the privacy of their home and not aired in front of all their guests."

For all her faults, my mother was a stickler for good behaviour, and she must have known Lady Belling would soon regret her outburst.

"Come now, Letitia," she said briskly. "You can quarrel with your son after the party. For all we know, the odious writer of The Whispering Quill is lurking around amongst the guests at this party. Surely, you don't want to see your latest quarrel splashed all over that dirty rag."

Lady Belling took a breath so deep that for a minute, I was worried her impressive bosom was going to spill out of her hideous mustard-coloured gown. It was such a pity that money couldn't buy good taste, for Lady Belling had more than her share of the former and absolutely nothing of the latter. Maria Bocelli, on the other hand, was exactly as beautiful as Bingo had described her. She was dressed in a beautiful emerald-coloured frock that floated around her as she walked towards us, her blond hair making a rather striking halo around her face. I didn't care for the amount of makeup she wore, but I supposed that was a professional hazard for someone who spent most of their time on the stage.

"Darling Bingo, won't you introduce me to our guests?" she cooed, as she wound a shapely arm through his.

Bingo turned red and gobbled like the silly goose he was before he pulled himself together and performed the introductions. Mother led Lady Belling away from our group on the pretext of speaking to a common acquaintance, and Bingo blew out a relieved breath.

"Show 'em the ring, darling," he said, turning to his fiancée rather proudly. "Your friend, Langley, put me onto it, Jimmy."

Jimmy and I shared a worried glance because Langley, the man who was planning to build mansion blocks on our lands, was hardly the sort of man we'd trust in matters of expensive jewellery.

"Erm, Bingo...old chap, I hope you got the ring valued before you bought it," said Jimmy carefully. "I'm sure Langley is as decent a chap as I've ever met, but he's certainly not a jeweller."

I tried not to roll my eyes at that blatant lie because there was nothing decent about Langley. He was the oiliest, most odious customer I'd ever met.

"Of course, I did," replied Bingo indignantly. "I showed it to the chaps at Cartier. They swore it was the real deal. A very rare violet sapphire surrounded by diamonds of the first quality. Cost me an arm and a foot, it did."

Maria held her hand out for us to admire the ring, and we had to agree that it was as beautiful as Bingo claimed.

"But how did Langley get his hands on such an expensive ring?" I asked sceptically.

Knowing Victor Langley, I wouldn't be surprised if the ring were stolen.

"It wasn't his, of course. He merely knew of someone who was in a hurry to get rid of it."

"Oh, Bingo! Didn't you even wonder why the owner was so eager to be rid of such a beautiful ring?" I asked in exasperation.

"Because it is cursed," said Maria dramatically.

CHAPTER 3

She looked as if she meant it, and I had to do my best not to burst out laughing. Because it was so patently absurd. Clearly, my brother did not think so.

"Cursed?" asked Jimmy, looking goggle-eyed.

Maria nodded, her expression a mix of excitement and horror.

"It is said that this ring brings misfortune to whoever wears it," she said with relish.

"If that is true, I'm surprised you agreed to wear it," I pointed out.

"No such thing as a hoax, Kitty. It's just a story," said Bingo.

"A legend," corrected Maria. "And I know it isn't true, but one can only hope."

I stared at her in disbelief.

"Surely you don't mean you want to die?"

"Oh no! I don't mean for *me* to die. Of course not! But if the legend were even slightly true, wouldn't it be a sad misfortune if something bad happened to someone very near and dear to us?" she asked pointedly, looking in Lady Belling's direction.

It wasn't often that I was struck speechless, but what did one say to a woman who had just wished her future mother-in-law dead? I looked from her to Bingo, who was looking embarrassed.

"Come now, darling. You don't mean that," he said, with an uncomfortable laugh.

"Don't I?" she asked darkly. "We'd be rid of her for good, Bingo Bellums. Just think how wonderful it would be to wake up one morning and not have to listen to her telling you you're eating your porridge all wrong."

She took one look at our scandalised faces and burst into laughter.

"Oh, look at all your faces! White as ghosts, you are. I was joking. Of course, I don't want your mother to die, Bellikins. I want her to live forever so she can tell you to sit up and stop slurping your soup every single day for the rest of your life," she cooed.

Bingo turned a sickly shade of green, and I didn't know if it was at Maria's vicious words or at the prospect of being nagged by his mother for the rest of his life. He caught his mother's eye across the room, and she gave him an imperious nod.

It was time to announce the engagement. Bingo gave a nervous, rambling little speech about how he looked forward to a wonderful life with his beautiful Maria, while his mother and his fiancée stared daggers at each other behind his back.

We raised our glasses to the happy couple, and I heaved a sigh of relief when the orchestra began to play, signalling a start to the dancing.

The guests at the party were a curious mix of the Belling family's friends and Maria's. There were the usual suspects, of course, like Reggie Trentham, Gertie Dacre and her fiancé, the Duke of Girton. I also saw Lord Huntley, my mother's most determined suitor, in deep conversation with the stuffy old Lord Biddlecombe, who used to be part of my father's hunting set until gout made it rather difficult for him even to sit astride a horse, let alone gallop after a fox.

I saw Henrietta whispering in a corner with Prudence Sharp, Lady Belling's companion, while Bingo's long-suffering secretary, Basil Perkins, plied them with fruit cups. Just then, Lady Belling threw herself onto a chair near them and called out to Prudence in a waspish tone, and her poor, beleaguered companion set down her fruit cup and hurried to attend to her.

"I say!" exclaimed Jimmy in my ear. "Did you know there is to be a dance exhibition tonight? Bingo's hired dancers from the Café de Paris on Coventry Street. They will also be dancing with the guests. Getting this extremely dull party to liven up."

"You don't say," I replied absently, craning my neck to see who else I could recognise. "Jimmy, who is that woman dressed in scarlet?"

"The one with the frightening bunch of feathers in her hair? I dunno," he replied. "Do you think that hat is supposed to double as a bird's nest?"

He put out a hand and caught Bingo, who was walking past us just then.

"I say, old boy, do introduce us to your new friends!"

"Er...they are Maria's friends," replied Bingo. "And dashed if I remember any of their names! Although I think that woman with the bird on her head is called Bertha or Gerta or something. She's Maria's understudy at the opera."

"And who is the man dancing with Maria right now?" I asked.

"Oh, my aunt! Oh, my sainted aunt," said Bingo despairingly. "She's doing the Charleston! Mother hates the Charleston. She thinks it is extremely unbecoming, which is why Maria promised to stick to the tango and foxtrot tonight. Do you think she's doing this on purpose? To wind Mother up?"

I wisely held my tongue, but it did seem as if Maria was doing her best to get under Lady Belling's skin and going by the prodigious scowl on Bingo's mother's face, she was succeeding.

With a wicked grin aimed at poor Bingo, she threw decorum to the wind, spinning, slicing her arms, swivelling her knees, kicking up her heels in defiance. Lady Belling sat as if turned to stone. Meanwhile, Maria kicked one foot into the air and laughed joyfully as Bingo whimpered under his breath. The guests clapped loudly as the dance came to an end, and Maria's friends swarmed around her.

I watched as her dance partner drew her away from the group and led her towards the refreshments room.

"Bingo, who was Maria's dance partner?" I asked curiously.

"That was Sidney Bellamy, one of the lead dancers at the Café de Paris. If you'll excuse me, my mother's beckoning to me. Although at this point, I'd rather swim through crocodile-infested waters than deal with her," he said feebly.

Jimmy clapped him on the shoulder in sympathy and sent him off to face his mother's ire, while I slowly made my way to the refreshments room. I knew it was rather beastly of me to spy on Maria, but there was something very…proprietary…about the way Sidney Bellamy took her by the hand and led her away.

CHAPTER 4

The refreshments room was very crowded, but I managed to catch a glimpse of Maria's frock as she slipped out of the door at the other end.

I made my way through the crowd and had a narrow escape when old Col. Peters with the shaky hands spilled his glass of wine. I sidestepped it neatly and pretended not to hear stuffy old Charles Frobisher inviting me to dance with him. Even if I weren't on a mission to discover what Maria was up to, I'd rather languish in a corner with the rest of the wallflowers than dance with Charles, whose idea of good conversation was a lecture on the benefits of linseed mash over barley for his beloved racehorses.

I paused outside the door that Maria had slipped through and pulled it open just a little. To my surprise, I heard raised voices. I recognised one as Maria's and presumed the other was Sidney's. A quick peek around the open edge of the door told me I was correct. But what on earth could they be arguing about?

"You cannot do this to me, Maria. You cannot pick that blundering buffoon over me," declared Sidney angrily.

"Oh, don't be such a bore, Sidney! Why on earth would I marry you when I could have an earl?" asked Maria.

"But I've loved you ever since I set eyes on you! And I thought you loved me too," he replied.

"Of course, I do! But not as much as I love money," said Maria sweetly. "Now, go back inside and dance with one of those pie-faced friends of Bingo's, and I'll make sure he tips you well."

"I'm warning you, Maria," snarled Sidney. "You'll be very sorry if you marry that rich fool."

"Oh, all men are fools. Even you," replied Maria, with a careless laugh. "And I'd rather marry a rich fool than a penniless one."

Oh dear! I was eavesdropping on a very personal quarrel, I realised with dismay. I took a hasty step back and bumped into someone. To my horror, it was Charles Frobisher.

"Ah, Kitty! There you are! I tried ringing you last week, but you were out. I suppose you didn't get my message," he said, preceding his words with an important-sounding harrumph. How I hated that sound!

I did get his message, but I had no intention of returning his telephone call very soon, for to do so immediately would give him ideas. Even worse, it would give my mother ideas, because in her eyes, Charles was a very eligible bachelor. She didn't care that the man was a crashing bore.

I fanned my face desperately, wishing I could run past him without a reply, but I wasn't as ill-mannered as that. So, I did what any self-respecting woman would do in my situation.

"I feel faint," I whispered, putting the back of my hand to my brow and leaning against the door weakly.

"I say! Would you like some punch or perhaps a fruit cup?" he asked in a panic.

"I don't want to put you to any trouble," I said with my most die-away air.

"Not at all," he replied gallantly. "Wait here, Kitty. I'll bring you some refreshment."

As soon as his back was turned, I pulled open the door and slipped through it neatly. Sidney had grabbed Maria by the shoulders and was shaking her angrily, but he dropped his hands as soon as he saw me.

"I'm…I'm sorry," I said in embarrassment. "I don't mean to intrude…"

"Not at all! Sidney and I are old friends," said Maria, with a nervous smile.

"Erm…yes. I think I'm wanted in the ballroom. Now, you think about what I've said to you, my dear, and don't make any hasty decisions," said Sidney, with one last menacing look at Maria, before he bowed in my direction and walked away.

Maria shook out her shoulders and pulled out a mirror and compact from her little purse. She shot me a sidelong glance as she powdered her nose.

"I'm sure you're wondering why Sidney appeared upset," she began mendaciously.

"Not at all," I replied curtly. "You don't owe me any explanations."

I wasn't interested in the lies I knew she was about to spin. Besides, what was there to say? She had thrown Sidney over for Bingo because an earldom trumped true love. At least, in Maria's opinion. And who was I to say she was wrong? That was the way of the world.

I regretted the curiosity that made me follow her into the refreshments room because now I was burdened with this knowledge that I'd rather not have. What was I supposed to do with it? I couldn't warn Bingo because it would break his poor, foolish heart. And who was to say Maria wouldn't make him happy?

"Please excuse me. I think I hear my mother calling me," I said hastily, wanting to get away before she forced anymore confidences on me, and made my way back to the ballroom.

Part of me felt I ought to warn Bingo about Maria's past, but another part of me felt it was wrong to interfere in what was most certainly not my business. And for all I knew, Bingo probably knew all about Maria's past. And if he didn't, I could only cause harm by telling him.

When I returned to the ballroom, the stage was set for the dance exhibition, and the guests were being shown to the small round tables that now dotted the room. I spotted my mother sitting at a table right in the centre of the room and threw myself into the chair next to hers.

"I don't like these new-fangled dances, Kitty," she said disapprovingly. "I find them very immodest."

Normally, I would have argued with her, but I was still unsettled by the scene I had just witnessed and was heartily sick of the whole lot of them.

"We don't have to sit through the dance exhibition, Mother. We can leave now, if you wish," I said promptly.

"There's Jimmy," she said, trying to catch his eye.

"It's no use, Mother," I said, with a grin. "He's far too taken with the dancers to notice us. I'll have to go over to him and check if he's willing to leave with us. Although I don't think it's possible to tear him away until the end of the display."

"Bother the boy! I hope he doesn't fall for one of Maria's disreputable friends," grumbled Mother, as I rose and made my way to where Jimmy was standing. He beamed at me when I tapped him on the shoulder.

"This is the best spot in the room, Kitty. You can see all the dancers up close."

"I'm sorry to disrupt your evening, Jimmy. But Mother and I want to go home," I said firmly.

"But...we haven't seen the dances yet. Bingo promised me they were spectacular."

"I'm sure they will be, but we're tired," I argued. "And I can't say I care for Maria's friends."

"Well, I'm not leaving until I've seen the dances," he said stubbornly, and I sighed in dismay at the mulish set to his chin.

Jimmy was being most disobliging, but when he was in such a mood, there wasn't much I could do to sway him because my brother hated being *managed* by his womenfolk. It only made him more set on having his own way.

With a sigh, I made my way back to the centre of the room and returned to our table. There was a slightly larger table next to us, with Lady Belling looking very stern and disapproving, sitting on one side, and Maria on the other. There was an empty chair between them, clearly marked for Bingo, who was destined to spend the rest of his life being torn between his wife and mother. Maria's friend, the one with what looked like a bird on her head, sat on her other side.

As the guests began to settle into their seats, Sidney Bellamy approached the table and held out a cocktail towards Maria.

"To new beginnings, my dear," he said suavely. "I think it is best to let bygones be bygones."

Maria smiled up at him through her lashes and raised an elegant hand to take the glass.

"A French 75? So kind of you to remember my favourite drink, darling Sidney. And I'm so glad to see you've come to your senses," she murmured and raised the glass to her lips.

But before she could take a sip, Bingo walked up with an identical cocktail.

"Here! What's the idea? Are you trying to steal my fiancée by plying her with cocktails, Sidney?" he asked lightly.

Maria let out a little trill of delight and, taking the second glass from Bingo, set them both on the table in front of her.

"Not at all," replied Sidney, with a glacial smile. "She's all yours."

He bowed slightly and walked away, his face set in stone. Meanwhile, the girl with the bird on her head watched the scene with avid interest, and as Sidney walked away, she leaned forward and murmured something in Maria's ear. Maria shushed her hastily and turned to smile at Bingo, who sat down between his fiancée and his mother.

The lights dimmed slowly, and we let out a gasp as the room went dark.

"Benjamin, I do not like this," cried his mother.

"Oh, do hush, Mama Belling. This is part of the show," said Maria rudely.

I held my breath, waiting for Lady Belling to flay her to bits, but there was a loud drumroll before Lady Belling could vent her displeasure at the younger woman's rudeness.

The stage lights went up, and Sidney Bellamy swung his partner onto the floor for the first dance display of the evening. My mother harrumphed in disapproval several times during the next few minutes, but I thoroughly enjoyed the performance.

When the music wound down and the first set of dancers left the stage, I turned to see Lady Belling's reaction. But she wasn't looking at the stage at all. She was glaring at Bingo, who was leaning towards Maria to whisper in her ear.

"Silly Bellikins," she cooed. "Of course, I'm going to drink the cocktail you brought for me first. But which one is yours? They both look the same!"

"Wasn't it the one on the left?" he asked in surprise.

"I'm not sure. I set the first drink down when you

brought the second one, and for the life of me, I can't remember whether I put yours on the right or the left of it," said Maria, with a giggle. "Silly old me! Well, I'll just drink them both, and you can pretend I drank yours first."

"Disgraceful," muttered Lady Belling, as the music started again with a sultry riff on the saxophone. "Where is Prudence? Why is the girl never where I need her to be?"

"She's sitting at a table at the back of the room with Henrietta, Mother," said Bingo. "I can ask a footman to bring you what you need."

"I need a glass of sherry, but nobody ever thinks of me," grumbled Lady Belling.

Luckily for Bingo, a footman swung by with a tray of drinks and placed a sherry in front of Lady Belling just in time. He moved to place a drink in front of Bingo, and Maria let out a squawk as he almost dropped his tray on her head.

"Be careful, you fool," she said furiously.

The footman, who looked very young, walked away with a hastily whispered apology, and we all turned back to the performance. A foxtrot followed the one-step, and then it was time for the highlight of the evening - the Charleston. It was a lovely performance, but the female dancer couldn't hold a candle to Maria's earlier performance, and we all knew it.

When the applause died down, the lights came up slowly, and the guests began to rise. I noticed Bingo bending over Maria, who had slumped down in her chair. It looked as if she had fallen asleep during the dance display. Bingo shook her, but she didn't open her eyes, and when he shook her harder, her head slumped to the side.

She wasn't asleep, I realised. Maria Bocelli was out cold.

Just then, Lady Belling let out a loud gasp and began to wail.

"She's dead! Oh, she's dead!"

I leapt out of my chair and went to assist Bingo, who was still trying to shake his fiancée back to life.

"Stop saying that, Mother," he snarled under his breath. "Someone call a doctor!"

Dr Bentley, Harley Street's most famous nerve specialist and particular friend of Lady Belling, stepped up immediately.

"If I might be of some help, dear Benjamin," he said gently but firmly as he moved Bingo aside and examined Maria.

A few minutes later, he shook his head and stepped back.

"I'm very, very sorry, but there is nothing I can do to help her. I'm afraid she's dead," he said sombrely.

The room echoed with gasps of horror. Meanwhile, poor Bingo looked as if someone had hit him over the head with a stick. Stunned. Horrified. Disbelieving.

"But…but…she was alive and kicking just now. And I mean that literally! She kicked me in the shins under the table when I was about to offer to bring Mother a drink," he said, sounding dazed. "How can she be dead?"

"It is that ring," cried Lady Belling. "I told you it was cursed! But you *would* insist on giving it to her."

"That's only because you wouldn't give me Grandmama's ring, Mother," he argued weakly. "Kitty, do you really think it was the ring that killed Maria? It was supposed to bring misfortune to anyone who wore it. And I suppose death is the biggest misfortune in the world."

I didn't know what to say, but what I did know was that this looked highly suspicious.

"Help me move her onto a sofa," Bingo instructed the footman, and I reacted sharply.

"No! You must not touch her! Nobody can touch Maria or anything on that table until the police get here," I said firmly.

“The police?” gobbled Lady Belling. “Why do you need the police?”

“Any sudden death must be investigated by the police,” I said grimly.

“Do you mean…” asked Bingo, blanching with fear.

“Yes, Bingo. This cannot be a natural death. I strongly suspect that Maria has been murdered.”

CHAPTER 5

Jimmy pushed his way through the crowd, and I beckoned him closer.

"Jimmy, run and telephone the police," I urged. "And ask for DCI Burton at the Yard."

"Lor', not another dead body," he groaned, before he took off, with Basil Perkins hot on his heels.

Thankfully, he had the sense to do as he was told. Any other man would have blustered around and perhaps muddied the scene of the crime.

For that's what it was - a crime. Maria hadn't choked on a cherry stone or something similar, for she would have been blue in the face in that case. And she was too young and healthy for her heart to fail without any reason.

The poor thing! She looked peaceful, as if she were asleep. And yet, she would never wake from that sleep.

As for Lady Belling's ludicrous claim that it was the cursed engagement ring that was responsible for this…I snorted in disgust that she would resort to superstition when the truth was staring her in the face.

Somebody had done this to Maria Bocelli. Somebody had murdered her.

I should have been thrilled at the prospect of another murder to solve so soon after the last one, as any detective worth her salt would be, but all I could feel was a creeping horror. The mystery of this murder did not excite me. It made me sick to the stomach. I pushed the thought aside immediately because Lady Belling's wails were getting louder by the minute. And the guests were moving ever so slightly closer. Soon, they would swarm around Maria's corpse out of curiosity. I shuddered at the thought of them trampling all over the evidence.

"Lady Belling, you must be quiet," I hissed. "Please! If that awful anonymous writer gets hold of this scandal, you will never live it down. Do you want to see a caricature of yours in the papers with the word murder in the headlines?"

"Ooooohhhh, people will gossip about this for years! We will never live it down," she cried, and I hushed her desperately.

I hoped my brother remembered to call Detective Chief Inspector Henry Burton at Scotland Yard. I had first encountered him when my friend, Jane, was murdered during a mock robbery at a dinner that turned to tragedy overnight. Although we had our differences, we had joined forces to uncover the killer. After that, when my family had hosted Prince Vikram and Princess Noor of Dinpore, an Indian princely state, Burton and I were forced to work together to find the princess's missing sapphire necklace and track down yet another murderer.

We might not be the best of friends, but Henry Burton was the first name that jumped to my mind when I saw poor Maria lying dead. If ever there was a man I needed on our side right now, it was him.

Ten minutes later, we were still waiting for the police to

arrive, and Lady Belling was still weeping loudly while Bingo shook his head in disbelief. He had some colour in his face, now that he had tossed back a brandy.

"It simply isn't possible, Kitty. She was just dancing the Charleston not too long ago. How can she be dead?" he asked plaintively.

"Here, now! What's this?" came a voice from beyond us, and we turned to see a police constable swinging his baton impatiently. "I was told there's been a murder in these premises."

"I asked you to call DCI Burton, Jimmy," I hissed at my brother, who had accompanied the policeman.

"And I did," he cried. "Look here, my good fellow. This is a matter for your higher-ups."

"I'll be the judge of that, thank you. If you would all move aside and point me to the body..."

"But who the devil are you?" demanded Jimmy.

"PC Peddle at your service, sir. DCI Burton will be along in a bit. Meanwhile, I am here to make sure nobody messes up the scene of the crime. And it wouldn't hurt the case if I were to make the initial enquiries, so to speak," he said, blowing out his moustache pompously.

"I cannot believe DCI Burton would send a police constable to investigate the death of an earl's fiancée," I said furiously. "He should be here in person."

"As I said, Miss, he will be here soon. And he did not send me. I was present at Scotland Yard when Sir James reported the death, and I took it upon myself to protect the scene of the crime from amateurs," he replied, with a severe glance at me.

I drew myself up with hauteur. How dare he call me an amateur?

"I beg your pardon?" I asked frostily.

"Aye, we've all heard about you at the Yard, Miss Goring.

Fancy yourself a detective, don't you? Well, you won't be meddling in this case, that's for sure. Not while PC Peddle is on duty. Now, please stand aside and allow me to examine the dead body."

I stared at him in horror, almost tempted to refuse him access to the crime scene. We needed DCI Burton, not this pompous, blowhard of a PC Plod! But he was the police, and we had no right to prevent him from carrying out his duty.

I stepped aside duly, and he approached Maria's prone figure sombrely.

"She's dead," he proclaimed, and I tried not to roll my eyes in contempt.

Of course, she was dead! We wouldn't have called the police otherwise.

"Do we know the identity of the deceased?" asked PC Peddle.

"That is…that is my fiancée, Miss Maria Bocelli," stammered Bingo, making an effort to pull himself together.

"And the wailing lady is?"

Lady Belling drew in a sharp breath at his words and miraculously stopped crying.

"I am Lady Letitia, the Dowager Countess of Belling. Look here, you buffoon! You cannot barge into my house without the slightest knowledge of who we are and…"

But PC Peddle cut her off rudely.

"Don't need to know the peerage by name to solve a crime, milady," he said, clearing his throat angrily. "All I need is evidence. And evidence suggests that somebody here is a murderer."

CHAPTER 6

PC Peddle's words were met with a collective gasp before we all began to speak at once.

"How dare you insinuate such a thing!" said Lady Belling.

"You're mad," exclaimed Jimmy.

"Did he just imply…" began Bingo, clenching his fists, but I cut him off.

"Don't hit him, Bingo," I said hastily, before Bingo could swing at the constable.

PC Peddle blew his whistle loudly and we fell silent.

"There's no call for all this shouting. I'm merely trying to do my duty. Now, you cannot deny that it all looks very suspicious. The deceased was seated at this table, surrounded by this very group of people, when she met her end. Am I wrong in wanting to know how that came about?"

"We might have been sitting next to her," yelped Lady Belling. "That does not mean one of us killed her, you fool."

"I'll thank you to be polite to an officer of the law, madam," PC Peddle replied severely.

Lady Belling began to protest volubly, and PC Peddle had to raise his voice above hers to be heard.

"What the devil is going on here?" came a sharp query, and I let out a little relieved breath when I spied the furious form of DCI Burton striding through the door. "Lower your voice, Peddle, and explain yourself immediately."

PC Peddle drew himself to his full height, which wasn't much, and cast DCI Burton an aggrieved look.

"I was merely performing my duty, sir. Meanwhile, these toffs insist on getting in the way."

"We're doing nothing of the sort," I retorted angrily.

I drew in a long breath to calm myself and turned my back on him.

"I'm very glad to see you, DCI Burton. We do not mean to interfere in the investigation at all…" I began politely, only to be interrupted by DCI Burton's snort of disbelief.

"Come now, Miss Goring. I know you too well to believe that," he murmured. "If I may request all of you to step out of the way while my men secure the scene of the crime, I will speak to all of you by turn."

His polite yet firm request worked where PC Peddle's blustering hadn't, and we moved away from the table where Maria lay slumped in her chair. Meanwhile, Basil, Lady Belling's butler, and two footmen kept the other guests at bay. They stared at us with avid curiosity, and among the crowd, I spotted Sidney Bellamy, who stared at Maria's prone form with absolutely no expression on his face.

DCI Burton and the police surgeon conferred with Dr Bentley before they performed a preliminary examination of the body, while we kept Bingo as far from the scene as we could. Burton looked grim as he approached our group.

"According to the police surgeon, she can't have died more than thirty minutes ago. And yes, it is a case of murder. Poison, most likely. Although we will know more after a detailed post-mortem examination. Who was the last person to see her alive?"

“I was,” whispered Bingo.

“And when was that?” asked DCI Burton.

“During the dance display. I was sitting right next to her, dash it! And I didn’t even notice it.”

“So you say,” said PC Peddle with a meaningful glance at DCI Burton.

“What do you mean by that?” demanded Bingo. “Do you think I killed her?”

“That is exactly what we’re going to find out, Lord Belling. Who killed Miss Bocelli, and why?” declared DCI Burton.

Just then, Maria’s friend with the large bunch of feathers in her hat forced her way past the policemen holding the crowd back and ran up to us.

“It is him,” she cried, pointing a finger at Bingo. “He killed poor Maria! You must arrest him.”

Burton ignored our furious gasps and turned to the woman.

“And who might you be, miss?” he asked kindly.

“I’m Maria’s closest friend, Miss Roberta King. And I tell you, Chief Detective Inspector, that you must arrest Lord Belling. He was trying to wriggle out of the engagement, and when she wouldn’t let him, he decided to kill her.”

“Ooooooh,” cried Lady Belling again, and promptly swooned, right into Bingo’s arms.

His legs buckled under her weight, and it took some help from Jimmy and PC Peddle before they laid Lady Belling on one of the chairs. I began to fan her while Springfield, the butler, ran to fetch Prudence, Lady Belling’s companion.

“That is a rotten accusation, and you know it, Gerta,” cried Bingo.

“My name is Roberta, you chump! And I will not be silenced. I heard you begging Maria to call off the engagement because you are a snivelling, spineless little coward who cannot stand up to his mother."

"That is besides the point," said Bingo stiffly.

"That *is* the whole point. In fact, that is what the police would call a very strong motive," she said, tossing her head in defiance.

"That is arrant nonsense," argued Bingo, but he was interrupted.

"The police will be the judge of that, thank you milor'," said PC Peddle. "Sir, I think we should take Lord Belling to the police station immediately and check for his fingerprints on the glasses on the table. That's how the poison must have been delivered, if it is indeed poison. In her drink."

"Of course, the glass has my fingerprints, you fool," cried Bingo. "I brought her the drink!"

"Ah-ha! So, you do confess to the murder!" said Peddle triumphantly.

"Thank you, Peddle. That will be all," replied DCI Burton.

Peddle drew himself up with great dignity.

"But...sir," he began, going almost purple in the face. "It is imperative that we apprehend the culprit at once."

"Well, you cannot accuse people without proof," said Burton.

"I'm merely trying to help, sir. It seems to me as if there is a conspiracy to cover up the truth."

"We don't *know* the truth yet," I pointed out, and Peddle scowled at me. I ignored him and went on. "I know you will need to interview all of us, Detective Chief Inspector, but Lord and Lady Belling are clearly too distressed to issue any statements at this point. They are still shocked by Maria's sudden death. Must we do this tonight?"

"They are all fakin' it, sir. I know the type," said Peddle. "Especially the lady."

"That's your opinion, PC Peddle, but you're welcome to

try and rouse Lady Belling. I assure you that you will get nowhere when she is in this state," I said, shrugging my shoulders.

Prudence scurried past me with a bottle of smelling salts, and Lady Belling stirred with a groan, but I had a feeling that she was going to faint as soon as she raised her head and saw the accusing looks on the faces of Maria's friends, directed at her precious son.

DCI Burton let out a pained sigh.

"We cannot possibly question all the guests tonight. Peddle, get one of the constables to transfer the body to the mortuary, and make sure you get the names and addresses of everyone who is present here. Request them to make themselves available tomorrow to give their statements," he said. "Lord Belling, I will see you first thing tomorrow morning. Please make sure your mother is available for questioning, as well."

He gave me a tight smile and went off to see to the proper removal of Maria's body while we followed Bingo out of the ballroom, with Lady Belling leaning heavily on Prudence's arm, scolding her for something or other in a quavering voice.

"Kitty, I refuse to be involved in this matter. I've had quite enough of murders," whispered my mother angrily, as I led her into the little parlour.

"For once, I agree with you wholeheartedly, Mother," I whispered back.

To his credit, Bingo put on a stiff upper lip despite the accusatory glances coming his way and informed his guests that they were free to leave after the police officers had noted their names and addresses. We stayed until all the others had left since my mother refused to leave her friend to what she called the angry mob. It was only after Maria's friends had left that Bingo sidled up to me.

"Kitty, you have to do something," he whispered anxiously.

I turned to him in surprise.

"Me? What can I do?"

"I dunno, but I did not kill Maria," he insisted.

"Of course, you didn't," I said soothingly. "You loved her."

To my surprise, he did not meet my eyes.

"Erm…about that…"

I let out a loud gasp.

"Bingo! Don't tell me that awful bird-hatted woman was right! Did you really try to call off your engagement?"

"Well, what else could I do? Maria and my mother were constantly fighting and asking me to take sides. And you know how much I value my peace."

"Bingo, the Quill was right about you when they said you have a spine made of sponge," I said severely. "You have just confessed to having the perfect motive for the murder!"

CHAPTER 7

He looked tortured as he paced up and down the hallway.

"I did not kill her, Kitty! I swear I didn't."

"Calm down, Bingo," I replied, but he shook his head.

"No! Did you not hear Roberta's accusation? Everyone believes I killed Maria," he said. "We need to prove that I didn't."

I knew he was right. Bingo might be a fool, but he wasn't a murderer. Unfortunately, while the rest of us knew that, in the eyes of the law, he was just as likely to commit murder as anybody else. And there was no denying that he had the motive.

Still, one thing was certain. If I interfered in yet another investigation belonging to DCI Burton, he'd string me from the rafters and leave me there for eternity. There was nothing I could do at this point. Nothing at all.

But poor Bingo was one of my oldest friends, and when he stared at me with those dumb, helpless eyes, I didn't have the heart to turn him down.

"Promise me you'll find a way to help me, Kitty," he begged, as we made our sombre goodbyes.

The drive back to Merivale Manor was mostly silent. I couldn't believe that the evening had ended on such a tragic note. I was about to go upstairs when my mother detained me with a hand on my arm.

"I've changed my mind, Kitty. We must all help Letitia and Benjamin get through this miserable time. One cannot allow one of England's oldest families to be thus disgraced. We must do whatever it takes to prove that Lord Benjamin Belling did not kill his fiancée," she said firmly.

Oh, bother! Now there was no escaping it. When my mother set her mind on something, she wouldn't rest until she had her way. She was even more implacable than Lady Belling. Still, I had to make her understand that I couldn't muscle my way into the investigation.

"Mother, if I interfere in this case, DCI Burton will arrest me even before he arrests Bingo."

"I'd like to see him try," she said with a militant gleam in her eyes.

"I wouldn't," I retorted. "But I will do my best to help Bingo. Although I have no idea what that might be."

"Go to bed now, and sleep on it," she advised, and I retired to bed.

I hoped the morning would bring me some ideas. But when Polly drew the curtains the next day and flooded my bedchamber with the late morning sunshine, I was no closer to a solution than I was the previous night. When I went down to breakfast much later than usual, I noted that Jimmy and my mother looked as heavy-eyed and tired as I felt.

Jimmy tossed his newspaper aside, and I noticed three others lying on the floor.

"Maria Bocelli's murder is all the newspapers can talk

about. Poor Bingo must be devastated," he said gruffly. "Who do you think did it, Kitty? Surely, it can't be our friend."

"Benjamin Belling could never commit murder," declared Mother. "He's far too squeamish to kill anyone. I've never seen him so much as squash a bug. I refuse to believe he poisoned his fiancée. It must have been one of those disreputable friends of hers."

Sidney Bellamy's face popped into my head immediately. Had he meant what he said about Maria being sorry if she went ahead with the wedding? He had claimed to love her. Was he so far gone in love that he would kill her before he let her marry another man?

I was picking listlessly at my kippers as I mulled this over when Romley cleared his throat meaningfully.

"Your ladyship, the latest issue of The Whispering Quill has just been delivered; should you wish to read it," he intoned.

"What's that?" asked Jimmy with a yawn.

I set my fork down and turned to Romley.

"Isn't that the rag that Lord Belling mentioned the other day?"

"Yes, miss," he replied.

"Well, bring it in, man," replied Jimmy. He barely waited for the door to close behind Romley before he spoke. "Do you think the anonymous scribbler has heard of our latest scandal?"

"I'd hardly call the murder a scandal, Jimmy," I said disapprovingly, just as Romley entered the room with the tabloid on a salver.

I leapt up and grabbed it before Jimmy could get his jam-stained fingers on it and waited until Romley and the footmen left the room before I shook it open. My eyes widened as I read the headline.

"Oh dear," I whispered. "You were right, Jimmy. Our

anonymous friend has heard about Maria's murder. Moreover, they've heard about Roberta King's accusation against Bingo."

"Give me that," said my mother, snatching the sheet out of my hands. She turned red in the face as she read the article. "Shameful! How dare they publish such drivel? We must tell Benjamin to sue them for slander!"

"It's not slander if it's true, Mother," I reminded her. "And I'm sure there are witnesses who will confirm that the scene described in the paper did take place exactly as they mentioned it."

"Do you think the writer was at the party?" asked Jimmy, as he reached for the sheet.

"I'm sure it is one of Maria's friends. That girl with the bird on her head - the one who accused Benjamin of murder - I am convinced it is her," said Mother firmly.

"We cannot make baseless accusations, Mother. Not unless *we* want to be sued for slander," I said just as firmly. "Besides, she didn't seem the literary type."

"I beg your pardon, Sir James," said Romley. "You have a telephone call from Lord Belling."

"Bingo? I wonder what's happened now," said Jimmy, throwing his napkin down as he rose from the table.

I followed him out into the hallway and listened shamelessly to his conversation with Bingo.

"Hullo, old chap! What ails you now?"

Bingo's voice was loud and carried enough for me to hear his side of the conversation as well.

"Jimmy, I cannot do this alone," he said. "Mother is very upset. My darling Maria's dead, and you can't turn around in this house without tripping over a blasted policeman."

"I'm sorry to hear that, old chum, but you have to let them do their job," said Jimmy.

"But I don't trust them to do it right," complained Bingo. "That PC Plod..."

"Peddle," corrected Jimmy.

"Yes, him...he's trying to pin this on me, while Mother has taken an awful dislike to the lot of them. Burton's here, asking to speak to her, but she refuses to come out of her room. What am I going to do?"

"Do you need us to come over for moral support?" asked Jimmy.

"That would be wonderful, thank you! And if you can convince Kitty to stick her nose in this business, that would be even better."

I grabbed the receiver from Jimmy with a glare.

"I beg your pardon?" I asked frostily. "I am not in the habit of sticking my nose into anything!"

"Erm...hehe...dash it, Kitty! You know what I mean..." he said defensively.

"Do I?"

"Awfully sorry and all that. Now, will you help out a friend in need? I don't trust this Burton one bit. And believe me, Kitty, when I tell you that my mother's doing her best to get me thrown into prison. Do you know, she set her Pekingese on PC Peddle? He chased the poor man all around the gardens, and now he hates us more than ever."

I tried not to laugh at the thought of that awful PC Peddle running around the gardens with Lady Belling's deceptively named dog, Pudding, trying to take a bite out of his backside. Pudding was a tiny Pekingese with the heart of a marauding beast, and he hated everyone equally, whether they were chimney sweeps or visiting heads of state. Just last year, he had bitten the American ambassador at one of Lady Belling's political soirées.

Still, I could understand Bingo's predicament. It wouldn't do to have his mother's dog attack a policeman when he was trying to stay out of prison. Besides, Bingo was hardly the type of man who had a firm head on his shoulders on the best of days, let alone now, when he was grief-stricken over his fiancée's death. He couldn't possibly handle this on his own. If ever there was a time when he needed his friends to rally around him, it was now.

"All right, Bingo. We're coming over to help you through this time," I promised.

"Pack a bag, Kitty. It would be best if you and Jimmy stayed with us until this blows over. I've got the inquest and Maria's funeral to get through, and I don't think I can do it by myself," he said gravely.

"This is hardly the time for a house party, Bingo," I scolded. "You'll be featured all over the papers for the wrong reasons again."

"Oh, this is no party, Kitty. Quite the opposite! You might have to form a human wall to keep Peddle from dragging me off to prison. Especially after the blasted cartoon in the latest edition of the Quill. Did you see it?"

"We did," I replied. "And it was awful."

"And that blasted Peddle has taken that to be evidence of my culpability, dash it!"

"DCI Burton won't arrest anyone without real evidence, Bingo. He's a very good policeman, and he won't allow Peddle to bungle the investigation," I promised. "But if you insist, we will all come and stay with you for a few days."

So it was that we packed our bags and drove to Grosvenor Square that morning, with Scottie firmly ensconced on my lap. When we arrived, the house was in an uproar. Pudding had been locked up in the little parlour and was barking his little head off in protest. Meanwhile, PC Peddle had set the servants' backs up with his insinuations against their master, and they were doing their best to be completely unhelpful to the police.

"This is obstruction of justice," Peddle snarled, while Bingo did his best to melt into the wallpaper.

"There you are," he said, with palpable relief when he saw us walk through the front door. "Kitty, can you please speak to Burton and tell him to take this madman away? I caught him badgering Mother's maid into letting him into her bedchamber."

"PC Peddle, I assure you, Lady Belling will be available for questioning by the police at four o'clock this afternoon. Do go away now and allow her to rest until then," I said quickly.

"Very well, madam. I will leave now, but I will be back soon. Lady Belling will have to answer her share of questions if we hope to get to the bottom of this case," he said pompously before Springfield showed him out.

"What an idiot," said Jimmy with disgust, as I gave Bingo the once-over.

He looked as if he hadn't slept all night. His clothes were crumpled, and his hair was askew.

"Is DCI Burton here?" I asked, wondering how I was going to explain my presence to him.

"I think he's interviewing the staff somewhere. I had a very painful interview with him this morning, Kitty. Do you know, he really believes one of us killed Maria! How ridiculous," exclaimed Bingo.

"Well, he's not wrong, Bingo. Maria was killed at her own engagement party. Which means that the killer was present at the party, too. But first, we must establish your innocence, so that the police stop wasting time with you and start looking for the real killer," I said briskly.

CHAPTER 8

I handed Scottie over to my maid, Florence, who promised to keep him out of everyone's way, and made my way around the house. When I ran DCI Burton to ground in the ballroom, a chill went down my spine as I entered the room that was now shorn of all the candles and flowers adorning it last night. It looked exactly what it was - a room in a house that was in mourning.

The large table in the centre of the room was still in place, although Maria's dead body had been removed, of course. DCI Burton sat at a mahogany table in a comfortable wing-back chair, facing the door. His brow furrowed when he saw me poke my head around the door. I waited until he had dismissed the second parlourmaid he was interviewing, and when she scurried out of the room like a frightened mouse, I walked in with a sheepish smile.

"What are you doing here, Miss Goring?" he asked rudely.

"I was a guest at the party last night. Don't you want to question me, Detective Chief Inspector?" I asked lightly.

"I will, after I am done with everyone at Belling House."

"Well, it seems I'm just in time then. You see, Jimmy, Mother and I are staying with the Bellings for a few days."

A scowl darkened his countenance, and I knew I had to tread lightly.

"I won't have it," he declared, and I couldn't resist a little smirk.

"This isn't your house, Detective Chief Inspector. We don't need your permission to be here," I pointed out gently.

"Oh, you can stay here for the rest of your life if you like, Miss Goring, but I know exactly what you're up to, and I'm not having it," he retorted. "You think you can wriggle your way into the investigation if you're on the premises, but I assure you, I won't allow it. As far as I am concerned, you are as much a suspect as anyone else in this house, and if you try to interfere with my case, you'll find yourself in chokey quicker than you can say Bob's your uncle."

"That is police intimidation, and I won't stand for it," I said indignantly.

"Well, this is a criminal investigation, and *I* won't stand for anybody interfering with it or trying to influence it to their advantage," he shot back.

"But I wouldn't dream of doing such a thing, Detective Chief Inspector. All I'm saying is that I know these people much better than you do, and it would only ease your way if I were to help you interview them. I could be your inside person, so to speak. As for being a suspect in Maria's murder case, what motive could I possibly have for wanting her dead?"

"Maybe you wanted to marry Lord Belling yourself," he said darkly. "He *is* quite a catch."

"Have you *met* the man?" I asked in disbelief. "He might be a great catch, but not for me. He'd drive me batty within the first week of our marriage! So much for your grand motive because I have no wish to be married to an overgrown schoolboy who trips over his own shoelaces."

If I could, I would have stuck my tongue out at him, but my mother had raised me to be a lady, so I did the only thing I could in such circumstances. I raised a very supercilious eyebrow at DCI Burton, and had the satisfaction of watching him grit his teeth in anger.

Then I remembered poor Bingo and his hangdog face and realised that antagonising Burton was not in Bingo's best interests. But before I could speak, PC Peddle burst into the room, waving a sheet of paper in triumph.

"We've got him, sir! The poison was in the drink!"

"What was it?" asked Burton eagerly.

"Cyanide, sir. By his own account, Lord Belling handed the deceased a drink before he sat down to watch the dance display. Now, all we need to do is match his fingerprints to those on the glass, and we've got an airtight case. Your friend will hang for this, Miss Goring," said Peddle with relish.

"I think not," I replied sweetly.

He turned to me in surprise.

"Eh? What's that?"

"I think you're getting a little ahead of yourself, PC Peddle. Because before you try to pin this on Lord Belling, you will have to answer one important question."

He blew out his moustache and gave DCI Burton a knowing look as if to say he was humouring the silly little socialite with cotton wool for brains. I had never wanted to kick someone in the shins as I did this man, but I restrained myself.

"And what would that be, Miss Goring?" asked Peddle, as DCI Burton frowned at me.

"Which glass was it?" I asked clearly.

Peddle blinked a few times in confusion.

"I beg your pardon?"

"Which glass contained the poison?"

I turned towards the table and pointed at it.

"There were two cocktail glasses on the table in front of Maria's chair. Both held the same drink. One was, of course, delivered by Bingo, but the other one was brought to her by Sidney Bellamy. Now, which of the glasses contained the poison? The one on the right or the one on the left?"

"Erm…I…umm…" stammered Peddle, as the scowl on DCI Burton's face grew darker.

"Answer the question, man," he snapped, and Peddle blanched with fear.

Burton muttered a barely audible curse and strode out of the room, while Peddle and I stared at each other angrily. Then, as one, we ran to the door. I elbowed the pompous little constable out of the way and caught up with Burton. Springfield was just showing him the telephone.

Burton dialled a number and asked for the forensic examiner.

"Stan, is that you? Burton here. My constable has just informed me that the cyanide was in the drink. Is that true?"

His brow furrowed as he listened to the reply, and he shot me a keen glance. I held my breath as he finally asked the most important question.

"Which glass was it in?"

DCI Burton looked grim as he replaced the telephone receiver.

"Well?" I demanded.

"The poison was detected in the remnants of the cocktail in both glasses," he said slowly.

CHAPTER 9

"Do you mean to say that there was cyanide in the drink that Bingo gave Maria, *as well as* the one that Sidney gave her?" I asked in disbelief.

"That is precisely what it looks like," said Burton, as we walked back to the ballroom.

"Then it is settled," I said, with a shrug. "Bingo cannot have poisoned Maria's drink."

"Why not?" demanded Peddle in outrage, as he tried to keep up with Burton's long stride. "Sir, I fear I must register a strong protest against a suspect being involved in the investigation."

"Use your head, man. Miss Goring had no motive for Miss Bocelli's death," said Burton irritably.

"So she says. But I am inclined to give her the benefit of the doubt," allowed Peddle, with ill grace. "Still, I hope you don't plan to entertain her preposterous suggestions, sir."

"There's nothing preposterous about it! It is a very simple deduction. I allow that Bingo could have poisoned the drink he brought Maria..."

"That's very kind of you," murmured Burton with a straight face, and I shot him a glare before I went on.

"...But it is highly unlikely that he could have poisoned the glass that Sidney brought. He simply did not have the chance to do that without being noticed."

"He could have done it under the cover of the dark," insisted Peddle. "I was informed that the lights in the room were turned down during the dance display."

"You are right in theory, Constable. But unlike me, you do not know Lord Belling," I said sweetly. "He's the clumsiest oaf in the world in broad daylight. I hardly think he's capable of dropping a full dose of poison into a drink in the dark without making a racket and knocking over every glass on the table. I am positive that if Bingo poisoned those drinks, everyone around him would have seen him do it. If you want to know what I think..."

"We don't," interjected Peddle rudely.

"That's enough," barked DCI Burton. "Please go on, Miss Goring. Tell us what you think."

"You should investigate Sidney Bellamy, the man who brought Maria the other drink."

"If Lord Belling didn't poison the second drink, Bellamy had even less of a chance to do it," pointed out Peddle. "As far as I know, he was onstage for most of the dance display."

Drat the man, but he was right! Sidney had been with his dance partner throughout the display and hadn't ventured anywhere close to the table.

"Maybe he had an accomplice," said Burton thoughtfully.

"Of course! He must have had one! But...who could it be? I was sitting right next to their table, but I didn't see anybody go up to them. Except..." I paused as something tickled my memory. What was it?

"I have been speaking to the staff, sir," said Peddle. "And they vehemently reject the idea of their master's culpability."

His words jolted my memory, and I clapped my hands.

"I've got it! There was a footman who served the table. But he only served Lady Belling and Bingo. He did not go near Maria at all, except when he almost dropped his tray on her head."

"What's that?" asked Burton sharply.

"It was just a slight accident. He was placing Bingo's drink on the table, and the tray almost slipped out of his hand," I replied, and Burton gave me an approving nod.

"You have a very keen eye, Miss Goring."

"Well, the drama at Bingo's table was simply riveting. I couldn't take my eyes off the tableau," I replied. "I wish you'd realise that I would be a very good asset in your investigation. I was sitting right next to Bingo's table, and I had a clear view of everything that happened last night. You and I might have had our differences, but you cannot deny that you couldn't have solved either Jane's murder or the mystery of the missing sapphire necklace without my help."

Burton rolled his eyes at my statement, but his craggy face softened a little.

"I wouldn't take it so far as that, but I will admit that you have been of help to me in the past, Miss Goring. Very well, I'm willing to let you in on the investigation, mainly because I don't want you sneaking behind my back and mucking up all my hard work," he said gruffly.

"That is extremely unhandsome of you," I retorted with a grin, and PC Peddle let out a loud, unhappy harrumph.

"Extremely irregular, sir," he muttered.

"Please allow me to be the judge of that, Peddle. Speak to the footman who served the table last night and find out what exactly happened with his tray."

Peddle gave us a stiff little bow and strode out of the room angrily.

"He's a very angry little man, isn't he?" I asked after the door shut behind him.

"I don't blame him," said DCI Burton. "The poor chap's desperate for a promotion, and you keep getting in the way."

"Me? What did I do?"

"Well, you keep showing him up in the worst light."

"Oh, dear. No wonder he hates the very sight of me," I murmured guiltily.

"He'll live," said Burton with an unsympathetic smile. "Now, I want you to tell me exactly who sat where last night."

I took him around the table and showed him where everyone was sitting.

"So Maria Bocelli was surrounded by at least two people who wanted her dead," said Burton.

"Who?" I asked in surprise.

"Lord Belling and his mother."

"I know these people, Detective Chief Inspector. They are not murderers. Lady Belling might flay you with her tongue, but she wouldn't go so far as to poison the woman her son claims to love. For all her faults, she *is* a loving mother, even if she's a tad too domineering for my taste. As for Bingo… you've met the man. Do you think he is smart enough to pull off such a murder?"

"You'd be surprised what people are capable of doing when they are cornered, Miss Goring," he replied. "And you cannot deny that Lord Belling was as cornered as can be. He did not wish to marry Miss Bocelli anymore, but she wouldn't break off the engagement."

"We only have Roberta King's word for that," I reminded him.

"Was she in Miss Bocelli's confidence?"

"All I know is that she was Maria's understudy at the opera," I replied with a shrug. "Detective Chief Inspector, we must consider the only other person who had both motive and opportunity, and that is Sidney Bellamy."

CHAPTER 10

"Why would Mr Bellamy want to kill Miss Bocelli?" asked Burton in exasperation.

"Because he loved her! And he was furious about her engagement to Bingo."

I hastily told him all that I had overheard between the two of them last night.

"He swore he would make her sorry if she went ahead with this marriage, and he kept his word," I said softly.

"But what about the second cocktail? How did he manage to poison that one as well? And why would he do that if he had already poisoned one drink?"

"Maybe he was worried she would only drink one, and he didn't want to take any chances."

"Yes, but how did he do it?" asked Burton.

"As we discussed earlier, maybe he had an accomplice. I wouldn't put it past him to bribe a footman into dropping a bit of cyanide in the second glass," I insisted.

"And how did the footman know which glass to drop it in?" asked Burton, his voice dripping with scepticism. "After all, both glasses were identical."

"Let us find him and ask him, by all means," I suggested. "I'm sure PC Peddle has managed to round him up by now."

But when we stepped out into the hallway, we were met with absolute chaos. Far from interviewing a footman, PC Peddle was clinging precariously to the top of the enormous, solid mahogany hall stand with coat hooks and umbrella holders that took pride of place in the hallway, and it was in danger of toppling over, taking him with it. It didn't take a genius to understand why he was perched on the hall stand like a human gargoyle snarling at the world below him, because Lady Belling's dog, Pudding, and my Scottie seemed to have ganged up on him, and prowled around the base of the stand like two miniature lions who had treed a cheetah in the Serengeti.

"Away, you pests," snarled Peddle, trying to shoo them away with one hand. "Go away!"

"Scottie," I cried in horror, and pounced on him, dragging him away by the collar. "Get down, you beast!"

Meanwhile, Springfield used a leg of mutton to tempt Pudding away from Peddle's feet, which were desperately scrabbling for purchase on the stand.

Both the dogs protested vociferously at being cheated of their prey, but we managed to shut them into the little parlour to fight over the leg of mutton in peace. A footman helped Peddle climb down from the stand, and we ignored the fact that he looked rather the worse for wear as he stood at rigid attention.

When he had composed himself enough to speak, he turned to me in fury.

"That dog is a menace to society, madam," he snarled. "I should have both of you arrested and thrown into gaol immediately."

"Easy, Peddle," warned DCI Burton.

"I'm awfully sorry, Constable. I assure you, I will give Scottie a sound telling off for his bad behaviour," I said contritely, and he huffed in response.

"Now, did you find that footman, or did you spend all your time playing fetch with the dogs?" asked Burton irritably.

I felt sorry for the poor constable. After all, it wasn't his fault Pudding was such a little menace, and Scottie was a little idiot who could never resist a chase. But Peddle was only doing his job and did not deserve to be raked down for being chased around by the beasts.

"I haven't had a chance to speak to anyone yet because of the wild animals that attacked me, sir," he replied, with an aggrieved look at me.

"Allow me to make up for my dog's bad behaviour, Constable," I said meekly, before I hailed the butler, who was waiting patiently by the green baize door that led below stairs.

"Springfield, we must speak to the footman who served Lord and Lady Belling their drinks during the dance display last night, just before we found Miss Bocelli dead."

He bowed and retreated behind the green baize door to do the needful. Meanwhile, I skipped upstairs to convince Lady Belling to speak to DCI Burton. Prudence let us into the dowager countess's imposing sitting room rather reluctantly. The room was done up in the same ghastly shades of gold as the ballroom.

My mother was keeping her company over tea and crumpets, and Bingo paced up and down the room worriedly.

"DCI Burton would like to speak to you, Lady Belling," I said firmly, and she turned an angry purple.

"We have done nothing wrong, Kitty. It isn't our fault Maria died in our house, and I will not be treated as a common criminal," she said, and DCI Burton let out an exasperated sigh.

I didn't know why I felt the need to rush to his defence.

"I assure you, Lady Belling, DCI Burton will treat you with the utmost respect. As you might have heard, I've had the pleasure of working with him in the past, and he is nothing but a complete professional."

Burton stared at me in surprise and raised a quizzical eyebrow, and I flushed, feeling as if my foolish defence of him was uncalled for and unwanted.

"Miss Goring is too kind," he murmured. "You have nothing to worry about, Lady Belling. I'm merely trying to get to the truth in this case."

"But how can I be sure you won't try to pin this on my son?" she demanded.

"This is a police investigation, ma'am. Not a witch hunt," he replied severely.

"It is just a formality, Mother," said Bingo.

But DCI Burton shook his head immediately.

"I'm afraid that this is much more than a formality, Lord Belling. Miss Bocelli was poisoned, and the forensic investigation found traces of the poison in her drink. Somebody at the table poisoned your fiancée," he said. "If you do not cooperate with me, I will conclude that you have something to hide, and you will be as much of a suspect in the case as your son."

Lady Belling looked outraged at the thought of being called a suspect, and she set her chin stubbornly. She wasn't used to being thwarted, and I hid a smile at the thought that DCI Burton was about to discover this the hard way.

"This is police brutality," she exclaimed, all chins wobbling in anger. "I will not have it. Not in my house!"

But Burton seemed to be a match for her.

"Asking you a few pertinent questions is not brutality,

ma'am," he said dryly. "Nobody is above the law. Not even the Dowager Countess of Belling, or her son."

"Letitia, you must allow the police to do their job," said my mother, putting a hand on Lady Belling's shoulder in warning. "Otherwise, it will be considered an obstruction of justice. You don't want them to get any ideas, do you?"

Lady Belling heeded my mother's warning and tossed her head haughtily.

"Very well. I shall not stand in the way of justice, but I do not like this. At all. Benjamin, I am extremely unhappy," she declared, and Bingo blanched at his mother's ominous words.

DCI Burton merely gave her a glacial smile and sat down on the sofa across from her wingback chair.

"Now, Lady Belling, please tell me everything you saw last night."

"There isn't much to say, Detective Chief Inspector. It was the cursed engagement ring that killed my son's fiancée."

"I beg your pardon?"

"My foolish son insisted on buying her a ring that is infamous for bringing misfortune to everyone who wears it. I told him not to buy it, but he wouldn't listen to me. And now, we're having to pay the price for his stubbornness," she said, with a sob.

DCI Burton stared at her in disbelief.

"Lady Belling, let me assure you that it isn't a ring or a superstition that killed Miss Bocelli. It was poison. And the poison was put into her drink by a living, breathing person, who might have found it funny to exploit this superstitious tale to their own benefit. And if we hope to find the person who did this, I need you to forget about the ring and tell me exactly what you saw that night," he said sternly, and Lady Belling wilted in the face of his severity.

"That woman put up a disgraceful performance before

the dance display, and I had half a mind to retire to my room. But I stayed out of concern for my son. I could not leave him that woman's mercies. She had him wound around her little finger, so much so that he couldn't even remember to procure any refreshments for his own mother," she said, with an injured look at Bingo.

"Did anybody walk up to the table after the dance display began?" asked Burton.

"Only a footman, with our drinks," replied Lady Belling, confirming what we all knew. "I tell you, Detective Chief Inspector, Benjamin had nothing to do with Maria's death."

"If not him, madam, then who could it have been?" asked Burton. "In your opinion, who could have possibly killed Miss Bocelli?"

"I'll tell you who it was," snarled Bingo. "It was that rotter, Sidney! He brought her that drink, didn't he?"

"Interestingly, Lord Belling, there was cyanide in both the glasses," said Burton. "Maybe both of you decided to poison her on the same night. Now, I'd like to know more about what Miss King implied. Did you really try to break off your engagement with Miss Bocelli?"

"Well…I…er…I had no choice, Detective Chief Inspector. Maria simply did not get along with my mother, and I was tired of the constant fighting," replied Bingo. "I merely told her maybe it was time to think again if we were suited to each other."

"And how did she react when you said that?"

"She threw a china ornament at my head," said Bingo, and I winced in sympathy. "It left a little bump on my noggin."

"And that made you so angry that you decided to poison her," murmured Burton.

"What? No, dash it! I wouldn't know how to go about poisoning anybody," cried Bingo.

Lady Belling protested volubly against this accusation against her son. Meanwhile, my mother and Prudence watched the proceedings with avid interest.

"What about the rest of you?" asked Burton. "I'd like an account of what you were all doing when Miss Bocelli was killed."

"I was watching the dance display," said Lady Belling promptly.

"As was I," chimed in my mother.

"And Miss Sharp?"

"I was doing the same, Detective Chief Inspector," said Prudence, jumping like a scared rabbit.

"Yes, you were watching the dances when you should have been bringing me some refreshments," snapped Lady Belling. "She is a most lazy and inefficient companion."

Prudence coloured guiltily, and I gave her a sympathetic smile. It wasn't easy to deal with Lady Belling. But Prudence had to put up with her because she had nowhere to go.

"And what about Lord Belling's secretary?" asked Burton, consulting his notebook. "Basil Perkins?"

"Come to think of it, where *was* Basil during the dance display?" asked Bingo in confusion. "I bet he was slacking off and helping himself to fruit cups when he should have been keeping an eye on that dastardly Sidney Bellamy."

"Lord Belling, who was the footman who served your drinks last night? From what I gather, he almost dropped his tray on Miss Bocelli's head," said Burton, after he made a note in his notebook.

"I dunno. You'll have to ask Springfield," replied Bingo.

"Did you not recognise him?"

"Never saw his face," said Bingo with a shrug.

"We only employ the best servants available, Detective Chief Inspector," said Lady Belling stiffly. "And they know how to make themselves invisible. Now, will you go and investigate this other man, Bellamy, or are you going to try and pin the murder on Benjamin out of sheer laziness?"

"Fear not, Lady Belling. If your son is convicted of his fiancée's murder, it will be based on sheer evidence, and not out of any prejudice on my part," replied Burton bitingly.

CHAPTER 11

Bingo whimpered with fear as Burton rode and strode out of the room.

"Do something, Kitty! I don't want to hang for a crime I did not commit," he cried.

"Don't be silly, Bingo. You cannot be convicted without evidence, and there isn't a shred of evidence to connect you to the crime," I said bracingly, before I paused. "Is there?"

"Of course not!"

"All right, then. Stop quaking in your boots at the sight of the police. Meanwhile, I'm going to make sure we investigate everybody who was present in the ballroom last night. And I assure you, I won't rest until we've found Maria's killer."

I rose from my chair and followed Burton out of the room, leaving my mother and Prudence to get on with the task of restoring Lady Belling with some more tea and crumpets.

DCI Burton was speaking to the butler when I went downstairs, with a frown darkening his face.

"What do you mean you can't find him?" he demanded angrily.

Springfield shrugged lightly.

"I assure you, sir. I have spoken to every footman under me, and they all say they did not serve at Lord Belling's table during the dance display," he said.

"That's nonsense," I said sharply. "I did see a footman serving the table."

"As did I, miss," replied Springfield. "But the lights were turned down, and I was standing by the door, too far to see who it was. And none of the footmen will own up to being the one who served that table."

"They have nothing to fear, Springfield," I said.

"There are four footmen in the house, miss. With tables dotted all over the room, they each had a designated area to serve during the show," he began, and Burton shook his head impatiently.

"Well, which of them was it that served the Belling's' table?"

"The first footman, of course, sir. But he says he didn't go near the table during the dance display because there was already a footman serving their drinks."

"Summon this man at once," ordered Burton.

The first footman looked shaken when he arrived to speak to us.

"State your name, please," said DCI Burton. "Rodney Miller, sir. But the first footman at Belling House is always called John, so Her Ladyship doesn't have to remember all our names."

"I beg your pardon?" asked Burton in confusion, and he hastened to explain.

"Lady Belling does not remember the names of her footmen and maids. Hence, the first footman is always called John, the second Will. She does not deign to speak to the others, of course. And the first parlourmaid is always called Lizzie, and the second Flossie. We consider them titles rather than names, sir."

DCI Burton and I shared a disapproving glance at his statement. Lady Belling still clung to the abhorrent ways of old when servants were treated worse than dogs. She probably remembered her dogs' names better than those of the people who served her with such loyalty.

"I, however, shall call you by your given name," said Burton firmly. "Now, tell me what happened last night, Miller. You were supposed to serve at Lord Belling's table?"

"Yes, sir. But as I was doing the rounds of the tables assigned to me, I realised that there was another footman with a tray of drinks at the ready."

"Do you remember what he looked like?" asked Burton, but Miller shook his head.

"I'm afraid not, sir. I was too far away to see him clearly."

Burton dismissed the footman and turned to the butler.

"Springfield, do you think it could have been Miller, serving at the table?"

"As I said, sir. I was too far away to tell. And the lights were turned down in the ballroom during the performance. It could have been anybody."

"But why would Miller lie if it was indeed him?" I asked.

"Because the footmen were instructed to only serve the tables when the lights went up between performances, miss. To prevent accidental spillage of drinks," replied Springfield.

"Which is exactly what happened. The footman almost spilled his tray of drinks," I murmured.

"Indeed. And whoever it was knows that if he were caught making such a big mistake, he'd be demoted immediately, or even discharged from service. Lady Belling does not tolerate sloppy service."

"Do you know what this means, Miss Goring?" asked Burton.

"Miller could be lying to save his job," I replied glumly.

"Precisely! Now, shall we abandon the mystery of the footman's identity for now, and focus on the actual suspects?"

"Yes, please! I think it's time we spoke to Sidney Bellamy."

"We will speak to him, but I first want to speak to Miss Roberta King. She is strongly convinced of Lord Belling's culpability. I want to know if she saw something."

PC Peddle brought the police car around, and we set off for the Royal Opera House in Covent Garden. The sight of its neoclassical façade always gave me a little thrill as I remembered the many delightful evenings I had spent in the grand old building. During the day, the tall Corinthian columns and the large, arched windows looked almost ordinary, but at night, they were transformed into a magical palace with gas lamps casting a soft glow on the pavement outside. And the glamorous beauties who arrived in shiny motorcars, with diamonds sparkling around their necks, ears and wrists, simply added to the illusion of a fairy-tale palace.

Now, however, it looked empty and slightly shabby. Peddle pulled up outside the main entrance, and DCI Burton helped me out of the car.

"Park around the corner, Peddle. We won't be too long, hopefully."

Peddle drove away with one last aggrieved look at me. I felt guilty about cutting him out of the adventure, but I couldn't deny that the familiar thrill of the chase was coursing through my veins at last. I might have longed for a boring, uneventful life full of parties and picnics in the park, but I was made for more. I was made to hunt killers, rather than hunt for a husband, and I was immensely grateful for yet another opportunity to do so.

We walked past the liveried doorman and made our way backstage, into the rabbit's warren of narrow corridors lined with gaily coloured production posters, call sheets, and cast lists. We found the green rooms, but there was no sign of Roberta King.

Burton stopped a passing stagehand and asked him where we could find Miss King.

"She's the big star now that Miss Bocelli's dead, isn't she? Well, the first thing she did when she arrived this morning was to grab Miss Bocelli's dressing room. Didn't even wait until her friend was cold. You'll find her in No. 1," he said in disapproval, pointing us in the direction of the principal dressing room before he went on his way.

Burton knocked on the door of No. 1, and there was a slight pause before a voice bade us to enter.

Roberta stood in the centre of the room, with a dress in one hand and a blonde, curly-haired wig in the other.

"Miss King, I'd like to have a word with you regarding the events of last night," said DCI Burton.

Roberta gave him a misty smile that I did not trust one inch, and pulling out a handkerchief from her sleeve, dabbed at her eyes.

"I cannot believe our darling Maria would ever come to such a tragic end," she said on a choked sob that was blatantly false.

My dislike of her only grew stronger at this display of fake grief. She handed the dress to her dresser, who had a tape measure around her neck and a mouthful of pins between her lips, and the wig to another woman who was holding three other wigs in the same colour, but in different styles.

"CeeCee was Maria's dresser as well, and Birdie makes wigs for all of us. They are just as heartbroken as I am," she said, and one look at the two hard-eyed women told me she was right. They felt as much grief over Maria Bocelli's death as did the woman who claimed to be her best friend.

"I'm sorry for your loss, Miss King. But we'd like to speak

to you alone," said Burton, and the other women left the room with curious glances at us.

CHAPTER 12

Roberta King let out a loud sigh and waved us into two shabby sofa chairs, while she perched on the dressing table with her back to the mirror.

"I told you last night, Detective Chief Inspector. It was Lord Belling who killed Maria."

"Yes, you did say that. I'd like to hear about that in greater detail, if you please," replied Burton.

"Well, I'd like to hear why you've brought *her* along," retorted Roberta, pointing a red-tipped finger at me. "She's one of Lord Belling's friends, isn't she?"

"Miss Goring is assisting me with the enquiry," said Burton smoothly while I held my tongue and tried to keep my face blank. Roberta gave him a knowing smirk.

"Assisting you to quash the case against Lord Belling, you mean?"

"I would be very careful if I were you, Miss King," said DCI Burton frostily. "I'm a police officer, not a lawyer defending criminals. I'm here to do my duty, and Miss Goring is helping me get to the bottom of the matter."

Roberta King suddenly burst into loud tears and buried her face in her handkerchief.

"I *am* sorry, Detective Chief Inspector. I didn't mean to be rude, but Maria was so dear to me, and I'm afraid her killer will get away," she sobbed.

"Now, now. There's no need to cry," said DCI Burton gruffly, and I tried not to roll my eyes in disgust. Was he such a fool that he couldn't see through her playacting?

"It would help us immensely if you could tell us why you think Bingo killed his fiancée," I said sweetly, and Roberta dropped the handkerchief and the act. She glared at me for a few seconds before she turned to Burton and ignored me completely.

"It was right here, in this room, that Lord Belling begged Maria to release him from the engagement," she began dramatically, but Burton interrupted her.

"When was that, Miss King?"

"It was about a week ago. Lord Belling always brought flowers for Maria after her performance, and..."

Again, Burton interrupted her.

"Where were you when this conversation occurred?"

Roberta flushed uncomfortably and did not meet his eyes when she replied.

"I was in the green room on the other side of this wall. The walls in this part of the building are very thin. It wasn't as if I were eavesdropping on purpose!"

"Go on," said Burton mildly.

"Well, he usually brought an armful of red roses for Maria, but this time, he came with white ones. The thing is, Maria hated white roses, and he knew it. She accused him of not caring for her anymore, and he told her maybe she'd be better off not marrying him, since he did not see any way for her to co-exist peacefully with his mother. And then she called him a lily-livered, snivelling coward and threw something at his head."

I winced at the idea of Bingo being so foolish as to try and appeal to Maria's better nature. Of course, she wouldn't let him go. He might be the stupidest earl in all of England, but he was also the richest.

"Did you see what she threw?" asked Burton.

"No! As I told you before, I wasn't peeping through the keyhole. The whole cast heard their fight, and it was all we could talk about for days. Maria was furious, of course, that a chump like Lord Belling would think he could do better than her. That's when she forced him to announce the engagement, because once it was in the papers, there was nothing he could do but go through with the wedding."

"Didn't she want to marry for love?" I asked, even though I knew the answer.

Roberta King gave a mirthless laugh.

"But she *was* marrying him for love. She was marrying him for the love of money."

"And what about Sidney Bellamy?" I asked, and she gave me a shrewd look.

"Heard about that, have you?"

I shrugged in response.

"I can't imagine it was a big secret," I said lightly.

"Well, you're barking up the wrong tree. Sidney did not kill Maria. And I don't say that because I think he's a pattern card of good behaviour. He isn't. I wouldn't trust Sidney Bellamy with my grandmother in a dark alley, but he isn't stupid enough to risk his neck for a two-bit opera singer who liked to think she was far better than she really was," replied Roberta viciously.

"And that is exactly what this is," she went on. "A crime of extreme stupidity. Somebody was stupid enough to attempt to murder Maria in full view of a ballroom full of people."

"And yet, they succeeded," I murmured, and she shot me a look of severe dislike.

"That was sheer luck," she snapped. "Coming back to my point, I can think of only one person stupid enough and desperate enough to do something like that - Lord Benjamin Belling."

"Do you have any evidence to support your accusation, Miss King?" asked Burton, and she shook her head reluctantly.

"That's your job, isn't it?"

"What were you doing between half-past eight and nine last night, Miss King?" asked Burton, ignoring her comment and carrying on with his questions.

"I was sitting next to Maria at the table, and we were enjoying the dance performances."

"Did you notice anything unusual?"

"Well, just the incident with the clumsy footman, who almost dropped his tray of drinks on Maria's head."

"When did you realise Miss Bocelli was dead?"

"When Lord Belling cried out her name. I was riveted by the performances on the stage and hadn't looked at Maria for some time. But when Lord Belling called out her name, I turned around in surprise and saw she wasn't moving."

We thanked her for her help and took our leave. As Burton and I walked around the corner to where Peddle had parked the car, I turned my head and looked at him. He was deep in thought.

"One thing is clear, Detective Chief Inspector."

"What's that?" he asked absently.

"Roberta King might claim to be Maria Bocelli's best friend. But the truth is that she hated her. And I want to find out why."

CHAPTER 13

"Drive us to the Café de Paris in the West End, Peddle," said DCI Burton, when we climbed into the car. "I think it is time we paid Sidney Bellamy a visit."

"He won't be in yet, sir. From what I hear, he works the late dinner shift. He's one of their most popular and highest-paid dancers."

"Where can we find him now?" asked Burton.

Peddle held up his notebook with one hand as he held the wheel steady with the other.

"I have his address here, sir. He lives in Fulham Broadway."

"Well done, Peddle," said DCI Burton. "Take us there, please."

Sidney lived in a seedy little flat above a newsagent's shop, the entrance tucked between a row of grimy shopfronts. We went up the steep, creaking stairs and down a corridor that smelled faintly of boiled cabbage, and Burton rapped smartly on the door of flat number seven.

Sidney opened the door himself and scowled when he

saw DCI Burton, but the scowl turned into a smarmy smile when he saw me standing behind the Detective Chief Inspector.

"To what do I owe this pleasure?" he asked.

"May we come in, Mr Bellamy? We'd like to discuss the events of last night regarding the murder of Miss Maria Bocelli," replied Burton.

"And what is the beautiful Miss Goring doing here?" Sidney wanted to know.

"Miss Goring is part of the investigative team," said Buton curtly, and Sidney gave me a quick wink that made my skin crawl.

"Cosying up to the police, eh? That's one way to help your friends get away with murder," he murmured, and I had to clench my fists to keep from swinging at him.

"Or maybe I have a natural skill for catching killers," I said sweetly. "I *have* done it successfully in the past, and I'm sure I'll do it this time, as well."

That wiped the smirk off his face rather quickly.

"What do you want?" he demanded.

"We'd like to come in, please," repeated DCI Burton.

"You can talk right here," said Sidney.

"Or we can talk at the police station, if you wish," replied Burton smoothly. "I have the car downstairs."

"I'll have you know, Detective Chief Inspector, that I will be writing to the newspapers about the police brutality I have been subjected to since last night, while the police do their best to shield the real killer."

"Be my guest, Mr Bellamy," invited Burton with utmost politeness. "Now, will you let us in, or do I have to take you down to the police station?"

Sidney Bellamy's face twisted in an ugly sneer, but he stepped aside to allow us to enter his small flat, which was dimly lit with just one sconce on the shabby wall. I ignored the worn, mismatched furniture, the empty bottle of whiskey that sat next to a chipped teacup on a rickety table and turned my attention to the opera posters tacked crookedly on the walls. They all featured Maria Bocelli in different productions. Very telling, I thought, sending a pointed glance at DCI Burton as I sat gingerly on the ugly blue sofa that looked as if it hadn't ever been cleaned. Burton sat next to me, and Sidney threw himself into the matching sofa chair opposite us.

"Big fan of the opera, Mr Bellamy?" asked Burton, nodding his head towards the posters.

"Not at all," Sidney replied promptly. "Just a big fan of Maria Bocelli."

"I was given to understand you were slightly more than a fan."

"Now, who would say such a spiteful thing, Detective Chief Inspector?" he drawled, with a meaningful look in my direction.

I raised my chin and gave him a glacial smile.

"Indeed, it was I who informed DCI Burton of the scene I witnessed last night, Mr Bellamy. It did, after all, give you a very strong motive for her murder."

He leaned forward angrily.

"I adored that woman! Absolutely worshipped the ground she walked on," he snarled.

"Enough to kill her to make sure she never married anybody else?" asked Burton sharply.

"I might be many things, Detective Chief Inspector, but I am not a murderer."

"And yet, the glass containing the cocktail you gave her contained traces of cyanide, Mr Bellamy," said Burton, cutting through Sidney's bravado in one smooth stroke.

He blanched in fear and sat up straight.

"That's a lie!"

"No, it isn't," countered Burton sternly.

"Even worse, you're framing me for a crime committed by Lord Belling! I had no reason to kill Maria, I tell you."

"You threatened to make Miss Bocelli sorry if she went through with the wedding. I heard you say that to her," I pointed out.

"It's your word against mine, Miss Goring. I categorically deny making any threats against her."

"Your feelings for Miss Bocelli were no secret, Mr Bellamy," said Burton.

"Since when is loving a woman considered a crime?" retorted Sidney. "If you have any evidence against me, go on and charge me. You have nothing on me, and you know it."

He was right. If only one of the glasses had contained the poison, the police could have matched his and Bingo's fingerprints against the ones on the glass and solved this case much faster. But the poison being detected in both glasses had made the case much more complicated.

"Even if you say the drink I gave her was poisoned, you can't prove I did it unless somebody saw me do it," Sidney went on. "Meanwhile, if I were you, I'd look at the two people who were closest to Maria."

"Are you saying you weren't close to her?" I asked in surprise.

He gave a bitter laugh.

"If I were, do you think she would have gotten engaged to the most stupid earl in the country?"

"When did you first meet Miss Bocelli?" asked Burton.

"I've known her and loved her since we were children. We're both from Lower Slaughter in Gloucestershire. She was plain old Maria Burgess then, daughter of the village publican. My father was a blacksmith. Maria and I played together in the village green as children, and when we grew up, we shared the same dream of moving to London, where a grand life awaited us. Well, she fulfilled her dream, but I couldn't become anything more than a lead dancer at a nightclub. And that just wasn't enough for Maria. Especially when that aristocratic idiot showed up and showered her with diamonds and sapphires, something I could never do," said Sidney bitterly.

I felt a pang of sympathy for him because he sounded as if he did love Maria. But it also strengthened my belief that he had killed her, for sometimes, love was a stronger motive for murder than hate. Unfortunately for us, Bingo had had as much opportunity to kill Maria as Sidney.

"And what did you mean when you said we must look at the two people closest to Miss Bocelli. I understand Lord Belling is one, but who is the other?" asked Burton.

"Why, Roberta King, of course," replied Sidney.

CHAPTER 14

"Are you implying that Roberta King had a reason to want Miss Bocelli dead?" demanded Burton.

"A very big reason, Detective Chief Inspector. From what I've heard, they had a humdinger of a row a week ago. Everyone in the building heard them screeching at each other."

"What was it about?" asked Burton.

"Well, it seems Maria did not want to settle into tame domesticity after all. She wanted to be the Countess of Belling, of course, but she also wanted to be a star. She liked the adulation of being a prima donna and the rush of being on stage. Obviously, Lady Belling was horrified at the prospect of having her daughter-in-law sing on stage like a common trollop. Or so I've heard."

"That's why Bingo wanted to break off the engagement," I exclaimed.

"But how did this affect Miss King?" asked Burton.

"She was Maria's understudy, wasn't she? How could she become a star when the reigning star refused to give up her throne? Roberta felt it was extremely unfair that Maria should continue as prima donna when she was already marrying one of the richest men in the country. Why should she have everything while Roberta got nothing?"

"But they claimed to be best friends," I said in confusion.

"Come now, Miss Goring. Haven't you heard of the adage 'keep your friends close, but your enemies closer'?" asked Sidney cynically. "There can be no true friendship between a prima donna and the woman who is desperate to replace her. Their so-called friendship was just a way for them to keep an eye on each other."

"So, Roberta King did have a strong motive for Miss Bocelli's death," murmured Burton.

"And she had the perfect opportunity," I added. "She was sitting right next to her during the dance display."

"Please make yourself available for further questioning should we require it, Mr Bellamy, and I advise you to remain in London until this case is solved," warned Burton before we took our leave.

"Where to, sir?" asked Peddle when we climbed into the car again.

"What do you think, Miss Goring?" asked Burton.

"I'm dying for a cup of tea, actually," I replied with a grin.

"Take us to the nearest café, Peddle," ordered Burton. "Meanwhile, you can telephone the forensics team and chivvy them a bit about the fingerprint report."

"I've already done that, sir," said Peddle. "They said one of the glasses had Lord Belling's fingerprints, and the other had Mr Bellamy's."

"Does that not prove both of them innocent?" I asked.

"Not necessarily. It only means that neither of them touched the other's glass. But you do not need to touch a glass to drop some poison in it."

"Which brings us to Roberta King," I said triumphantly. "She had the motive and the opportunity. It would have been the work of a moment for her to lean over and drop the cyanide into both glasses."

"But we haven't a shred of evidence to pin this on her."

Peddle glared at me over his delicate, floral teacup, and I had to admit that if it weren't for me, he would be ensconced in a pub with Burton, discussing the case over a pint of ale and some pork rinds. But now, he was stuck at a table too small for the three of us, with a cup of watery tea and a plate of biscuits that were the consistency of cardboard.

It would have been evident even to the most oblivious onlooker that PC Peddle was deeply unhappy with my existence. Unfortunately for him, I didn't care. I felt terribly sorry for Bingo, but I was having a wonderful time playing sleuth.

I drained my teacup and set it down with a sigh and turned down the offer of another biscuit.

"Did you check Maria Bocelli's flat for clues?" I asked and was rewarded by an indignant snort from Peddle.

"That's one of the first things we did, Miss Goring. You're dealing with the police, not a bunch of amateurs such as yourself."

"That's wonderful," I replied, determined not to rise to his bait. "And did you find any letters?"

"Letters?" he asked, nonplussed.

"Yes, letters. Don't you think Sidney Bellamy would have written rather impassioned letters to his lady love to remind her of what they once had when he heard about her engagement? He seems just the type of chump who'd do that."

"Bah! It's always women who write letters," argued Peddle.

"And which detective novel did you get that information from?" I asked sweetly.

"Sir, this is unacceptable! Miss Goring is…"

"That's enough, Peddle," interjected DCI Burton, putting a

stop to his constable's tirade. "I will have a word with Miss Goring about speaking to you politely. Meanwhile, why don't you get the car out while I settle the bill?"

"Very well, sir. But where are we going now?"

"To Miss Bocelli's flat, man. To look for the letters," replied Burton, and I had to bite my lip to hide a smile.

Peddle gave me one last angry look and stomped out of the café after a smart salute that resonated with hurt feelings.

As soon as he was out of sight, Burton turned to me with a slight frown.

"That wasn't very well done, Miss Goring," he said gently.

"What did *I* do?" I asked indignantly. "PC Peddle is the most pompous ass if ever there were pompous asses in the world. He's..."

"He's also an officer of the law who's doing his duty, Miss Goring. He might not be the smartest match in the box, but he's very hardworking. He wasn't born into privilege, and he never had the opportunity for a fine education that could have advanced his career, but he does his best, and that is all I need."

"I'm sorry," I said immediately. "I did not mean to hurt his feelings. I will be more mindful of them, Detective Chief Inspector."

He gave me a warm smile that lit up his eyes and gestured to the door.

"Well, shall we go and look for those letters?"

As soon as I climbed into the car, I held out a hand to PC Peddle.

"I'm very sorry for my rudeness, Constable. I'm willing to be friends if you stop finding fault with my ideas constantly."

"Miss Goring," said Burton with a groan.

When Peddle gave him a reproachful look, he shook his head.

"You might as well be friends, Peddle. There's no escaping

Miss Goring when there's murder in the air. I've learned that the hard way."

Peddle shook my hand reluctantly.

"Very well, Miss Goring. And I apologise for my part in our arguments," he said gruffly.

"Take us to Miss Bocelli's flat in Soho, man. Quickly," ordered Burton, and Peddle sped away with a screech of the tires.

CHAPTER 15

Maria Bocelli used to live in a lovely three-bedroom flat on the third floor of a very fashionable mansion block just off Dean Street. The building had the loveliest wrought-iron balconies, polished brass doorknobs that gleamed like gold and a smartly dressed doorman who tipped his hat at us as he let us in.

Maria's red-eyed maid opened the door, staring at us suspiciously.

"Yes?"

"We'd like to have a quick look around once again, Agnes," said Peddle, and she allowed us into the flat, which was as theatrical as its late occupant. Velvet drapes in a rich plum lined the tall, sash windows. A grand baby piano stood by the fireplace, its top littered with sheets of music.

The mirrored sconces, lacquered tables and the hand-painted screen all screamed money. Maria might have had humble beginnings, but she had built a good life for herself here. It was a pity it was snuffed out so early.

There was a handsome mahogany writing desk in the sitting room and Peddle pointed at it triumphantly.

"That is the only writing desk in the flat, sir. And I found no letters in there."

"What about any secret compartments?" asked Burton.

"I did find a secret compartment, but it only contained money to the tune of one hundred pounds," replied Peddle.

I shook my head in disgust.

"Do you really think a woman would hide scandalous love letters out in the open?"

"Well, then...I can't wait for you to find them, Miss Goring," said Peddle, with a smirk.

I ignored the smirk and turned to the maid.

"Will you please lead me into Miss Bocelli's bedchamber?"

When I stepped over the threshold of Maria's bedchamber, I realised that bedchamber was a misnomer. This was a boudoir...lush, opulent, dramatic. The walls were papered in dusky rose damask, and a fringed chandelier cast geometric shadows across the high ceiling. The heavy velvet curtains were heavily drawn to shut out the world, and the huge mahogany bed in the centre of the room looked as if its owner had just stepped out of bed.

The bed was strewn with an assortment of pillows in brocade, lace and fur, and a garnet silk robe lay carelessly across the footboard. I looked around the room thoughtfully. If a woman like Maria had to hide some letters, where would she put them?

I looked at her vanity table, littered with crystal perfume bottles, rouge pots and pearl-handled brushes. There was nothing there. I rummaged through the massive wooden chest of drawers that stood in one corner, spilling clothes all over the room, but I found nothing. That's when my eyes fell on a large medieval tapestry. It looked out of place in a room that was decorated in Style Moderne.

I used all my strength to push it aside, and that's when I

saw it...a safe, built into the wall. I turned to Burton with a gleeful smile.

"I hope they taught safe breaking in your police academy, Detective Chief Inspector, because I am willing to wager my whole inheritance that you will find those incriminating letters behind that door."

"Well done, Miss Goring," Burton said appreciatively. "I'll call for a safe breaker immediately."

"But...you don't need to break the safe open when I can just give you the key," announced Agnes, and we turned to her in surprise.

"I beg your pardon?" I asked in confusion. "Do you have a key to your mistress's safe?"

"No, miss. But I know where she kept it," replied the maid. "Under her mattress."

She pointed at the bed and began throwing the pillows onto the floor. She beckoned PC Peddle to help her lift the heavy mattress, and when he held one end of it up, she fished under it for the key. She pulled it out in triumph, but just as Peddle was about to drop the mattress, a glint of brass caught my eye.

"Wait! Hold it up for a minute," I cried, rushing towards the bed.

I was right. I had seen a little knob on the inside of the bedframe. It looked like a decorative knob, but if so, why would it be inside the bedframe, rather than on the outside?

I grabbed hold of it gingerly, twisting it between my fingers until I felt it give.

"What is it?" asked Agnes eagerly.

"A secret hiding place," I replied, and she gasped.

"Open it," ordered Burton, and I slid the door open. To my relief, I found what I had been searching for - not one letter, but a bundle of them, tied with a velvet ribbon.

"And that's where a woman hides her scandalous letters,

Constable," I said with a grin, holding the letters out to Peddle.

"I think you've earned the right to open them first, Miss Goring," he said gruffly, and DCI Burton clapped him on the back in approval.

"Let's take them to the Yard, Miss Goring. And you can have first crack at them," he said.

Within no time, we were at Scotland Yard, ensconced in DCI Burton's office. I laid the letters on the table and undid the bundle carefully, with a frown.

"She didn't keep the envelopes. Why?" I murmured as I unfolded the first letter and read the contents.

My brow furrowed as I read it, and when I was done, I set it aside and grabbed the second one. Within minutes, I had gone through the entire bundle. My throat was dry when I turned to the two men watching me carefully.

"These letters aren't what we thought they would be," I said hoarsely.

"What do you mean, Miss Goring?" asked Burton.

"They aren't love letters. They are poison pen letters."

Peddle blew out his moustache loudly.

"Why would Mr Bellamy write letters of hate to his lady love?" he asked, and I shook my head in response.

"They aren't from Sidney. I don't know who sent them since they aren't signed. But they cannot be from him, because these letters were written by a woman."

CHAPTER 16

DCI Burton snatched up one of the letters and began to read in disbelief, while Peddle did the same. Meanwhile, I stared dumbly at the one in my hand. It was the most vitriolic piece of writing I had ever seen.

The anonymous writer at the Whispering Quill had mocked Bingo, Lady Belling and Maria in a purely entertaining way, but this...this was pure poison. Whoever wrote this filth must indeed have hated Maria. There were attacks on her person, her character, and even her talent. There were also threats that grew increasingly frightful with every letter.

The handwriting was not markedly feminine, but the emotion behind the letters was so. It was pure feminine envy and loathing. And there was only one woman I could think of who seemed to have hated and envied Maria Bocelli to this extent.

"If this isn't proof that Roberta King hated Maria Bocelli, then I don't know what is, Detective Chief Inspector," I said softly.

"That is a very dangerous accusation, Miss Goring," he

warned. "We haven't a shred of evidence against Miss King. All we have is hearsay. We've heard she was jealous of Miss Bocelli. But our source is Sidney Bellamy, one of the main suspects in the case, and hence, I would not give too much weight to anything he says."

I shook the letter in his face.

"Did you not read the letters she wrote to the woman she called her best friend?" I demanded in astonishment.

"And did you not notice they weren't signed? And there are no envelopes, which means we cannot trace where they were posted?" he argued.

"Sir, what if they weren't posted?" asked Pebble. "What if they were delivered by hand?"

"And who had better opportunity to hand-deliver letters to Maria than her understudy at the opera?" I asked.

"This is still all conjecture. We've *heard* she hated Miss Bocelli, and we *think* she might have written these letters, but until we *know* it as the absolute truth, there is nothing we can do," replied Burton firmly.

"What if we find a sample of Roberta King's writing and match it against these letters?" I asked.

"That would work," conceded Burton. "However…"

How I hated that word!

"However, we can't barge into her house and take handwriting samples by force. You need a warrant for that sort of thing, and we do not have anything against her that would convince the magistrate to issue a warrant."

I began to drum my fingers against the table, my mind racing with ideas.

"Well, what if you don't need to go to her house at all? We could find samples of her writing at the Opera House."

"We need a warrant for that, too," replied Burton impatiently.

"You do, but I don't," I said. "I can sneak into Miss King's dressing room while she is away and see if I can find something that connects her to these letters, and then, you can apply for a warrant on just grounds."

"But how will you explain it to the judge?" asked Peddle.

"We will find a way. You can blame it all on me, if you like."

"Oh, we will," promised Burton, with a rare grin.

"And when we solve the case, I'm stealing all the credit," I said, rolling my eyes at him as I rose from my chair. "When should I attempt to ransack Miss King's dressing room?"

"During the rehearsals tomorrow morning," replied Peddle, pulling out a piece of paper from his pocket. "This is the rehearsal schedule, miss. Roberta King's grand debut is scheduled for Friday night, and she will be busy in rehearsals all morning. Her afternoons are for dress and wig fittings, which take place in her dressing room, and her evenings are reserved for dancing and dining with the rich patrons of the opera."

"Won't her dressing room be empty then? I could try my luck this evening."

"I would advise against it, miss," said Peddle gravely. "The opera house will be full of the worker bees like the dressmakers, wigmakers and stagehands, and you will attract far more attention than is necessary. But if you drop in for an informal chat with Miss King tomorrow morning, you could stay in her dressing room until she returns from her rehearsals onstage."

"That makes perfect sense, Peddle. Well done," I replied, and was amused to see his cheeks turn a rosy red.

"Yes…well…" he broke off in embarrassment and saluted us sharply before he left the office.

"Well, Miss Goring, I think it is time to return you to

Belling House," said DCI Burton. "If you spend any more time at the Yard, we'd have to start paying you, and I'm afraid that after the budget cuts this year, Scotland Yard cannot afford to pay your consultation charges."

"I have a good mind to set up shop as a lady detective," I quipped as he held the door for me.

"That sounds like a wonderful idea," he replied, and I looked up in surprise because DCI Burton sounded sincere.

"I was joking," I stammered.

"But I wasn't," he replied.

For a minute, a wave of excitement came over me at the thought of setting up a real office and hiring my services out as a detective, but it didn't last too long. For my mother's furious face swam into my mind, popping the delightful bubble of joy that coursed through my veins.

Under no circumstances would my mother allow me to do something she considered common. Why, she wouldn't allow me to take up a job even when we needed the money. And now that our financial worries were behind us, it was simply unthinkable.

"It was a lovely dream while it lasted," I said sadly, but DCI Burton shook his head.

"Never say never, Miss Goring. The times are changing. Women are making great strides in a number of fields. You never know…maybe this time next year, I will be striding angrily into your fancy office in Dean Street to warn you to stop interfering with my cases as usual."

"If you do, I will be sure to tell you to…to…go and boil your head," I said, with a grin.

The next morning, I was dressed for the day when I came down to breakfast. Lady Belling and my mother shared a rather meaningful, but disapproving glance when they saw me.

"Where are you off to, Kitty?" demanded my brother.

"I'm off to save Bingo's bacon," I replied with a smile that I hoped was mysterious.

"Go on! Tell us how you plan to swoop in and save the day," he said around the eggs in his mouth, but I shook my head.

"Not yet, Jimmy," I replied, biting into my crisp, buttery toast. "Where *is* Bingo, though? I haven't seen him since yesterday morning."

"He's hiding in his room, convinced he's going to be arrested for the murder. I had to drag him to the club last night for our annual darts tournament because I had a lot of money riding on him since he is the reigning champion, but he put up a terrible show and cost me fifty quid," grumbled Jimmy.

"Jimmy, you didn't!" I said reproachfully.

"I did! And let me tell you, it still pinches me, Kitty. Fifty quid is a lot of money," he said, with a shudder.

"Not the money, you beast! I can't believe you took Bingo to play darts the day after his fiancée's death," I cried. "That is terribly bad form, Jimmy. Do you want The Quill to lambast the poor chap again?"

"Oh! I didn't think of that," said Jimmy sheepishly.

"You are a bad influence on Benjamin, James. Darts tournament, indeed," said Lady Belling stridently.

"Speaking of bad influences," said my mother hastily, trying to change the subject. "I meant to speak to you about that policeman, Kitty. You cannot spend so much time with him. I will not allow it."

"Hush, Mother! She's almost solved this murder case. Let her get on with it," said Jimmy. "You can lock her in her bedchamber after that."

"I don't see why you're taking such a personal interest in this case, Jimmy," my mother said in surprise.

"Out of sheer greed, Mother," I said dryly, as I rose from

the table. “He has no doubt wagered a large sum of money on Bingo at other darts tournaments across the country, and he wants to protect his investment. Now, if you will excuse me, DCI Burton will be arriving any minute.”

CHAPTER 17

This time, I walked into Roberta King's dressing room all by myself. I had checked the call sheet and timed it such that I knocked on the door just as she was about to be called out for rehearsal. DCI Burton was speaking to the manager of the Opera House, while Peddle was speaking to the other members of the crew, thus giving me the perfect excuse for being in her dressing room.

"Oh, hullo! I didn't expect to see you again so soon," she said in surprise.

"I wanted to speak to you about Miss Bocelli," I said. "To get an inside perspective. You did say you were her best friend."

"Of course, I was. Ask anyone here and they will tell you the same. We were practically inseparable. Now, if you'll excuse me, I'm late for rehearsal."

"Miss King, would you mind if I waited for you here, in your dressing room?"

She looked uncomfortable with the idea, but luckily, inspiration struck me before she could refuse.

"I'm meeting DCI Burton here later, and I know he particularly wants to speak to you again."

I knew Roberta King wouldn't resist the idea of speaking to the handsome Detective Chief Inspector, not after she'd spent all her time making eyes at him yesterday.

"Of course," she cooed. "Anything for DCI Burton. Birdie will keep you company while you wait, won't you, darling?"

She gave her wig maker a meaningful look before she hurried onstage, and the poor woman gave me a nervous smile as she sat down on a chair near me. Drat! How could I look through Miss King's personal belongings with Birdie watching me like a hawk?

But Miss King's reluctance to leave me alone in her dressing room strengthened my conviction that she had something to hide, and my resolve to find the evidence only became stronger. "Is there a powder room around here?" I asked.

"Yes, miss. It is three doors down to your right when you go out into the corridor," she replied.

I slipped out of the room with a mutter of thanks and made straight for where PC Peddle was speaking to a stagehand.

"Psst," I called, beckoning him over from behind a large cardboard tree.

"What is it, miss?" he asked irritably. "I still need to interview the costume department to see if they can throw any light on Miss King's relationship with Miss Bocelli."

"Did you learn anything of use?"

"From what I hear, Miss Bocelli liked to treat her understudy as a personal errand girl, ordering her about most days. And Miss King, naturally, hated her for it," he said.

"Excellent! I need your help in getting some time alone in Miss King's dressing room, Peddle. She's left her watchdog in there with me - Birdie, her wigmaker. I need you to create a distraction to get her out of the room."

"But...what can I do?" he asked helplessly.

"That is for you to decide," I replied. "Set fire to a wig if you have to, but get her out of the room!"

With that, I hurried back to Miss King's dressing room and found Birdie humming to herself as she repaired a large red-haired wig that looked more like a boat than a head of hair.

Within minutes, there was a knock on the door, and a sandy-haired stagehand poked his head around the door.

"Sorry to disturb you, Miss Birdie, but the manager is screaming his head off because he can't find the wigs for the three kings."

Birdie stood up with a gasp of horror.

"What do you mean he can't find them? I just brushed them out and put them in their dressing room an hour ago!"

The stagehand shrugged callously.

"Well, he says they aren't there anymore, and that heads will roll if they aren't found immediately."

"Honestly, I've half a mind to quit anyway," she muttered as she hurried out of the room.

The stagehand winked at me.

"You have about five minutes before she returns, miss. I hid the wigs under a chair, and it will take her that long to find them. I didn't dare take them out of the dressing room. That's more than my job is worth, even to help Constable Peddle," he said before he slunk out of the room, whistling softly as he went down the corridor.

I blessed Peddle's presence of mind silently and got to work immediately.

My natural instinct was to look in Miss King's purse, for surely, she'd have a notebook. I could tear off a page that had a handwritten list or a note. But Miss King's purse was nowhere to be seen.

"Silly, Kitty," I muttered under my breath. "Of course, she keeps her purse locked up in some cupboard."

I began to look through her drawers and found nothing. That's when I spotted the pile of music sheets scattered under a chair. I pounced on them and checked the name. The sheets did belong to Miss King, but they were printed. Darn it! Where was a handwritten grocery list when you wanted one?

Just then, Birdie came bustling in, and I groaned silently.

"They are all a bunch of fools, and Mr Gantry, the manager, is the biggest fool of them all," she grumbled. "It took me an hour to brush those wigs out, and *somebody* - I won't name any names - just swept them under a chair as if they were a bunch of scarves. I'm sorry, miss. I will have to ask you to wait in one of the green rooms because I have to go and post a bunch of letters for Miss King, and she doesn't like anyone being in her dressing room when she's not here. Miss Bocelli was the same. I'm sure you understand."

"Of course! I can see you're very busy today," I murmured.

"Yes! Miss Bocelli's death has cast us all into pandemonium. Miss King's first show is just days away, and everything has to be just right for it."

"I could post the letters for you, if you like. It would give you one less thing to do," I said slyly, and Birdie paused, looking very much like a little bird arrested mid-flight.

"Would you really do that?"

"Of course," I replied. "I was leaving anyway because I can see Miss King is too busy to talk to me today."

"It's nothing personal, miss. She's just been waiting so long for this chance that she wants everything to be perfect," she explained.

"I understand, Birdie. I'll come back some other day. Now, what about those letters? I can just pop them into the letterbox outside, if you like."

"Bless you, miss," cried Birdie, as she waved a bunch of letters at me. "Here you go. Mind you, post them right away because Miss King wants them to go out with the morning post."

"I'll pop them into the letterbox immediately," I promised, taking the letters and putting them in my handbag.

I thanked her and walked out of the room before she could change her mind. I found DCI Burton waiting for me in the lobby and gave him a brisk nod as I walked up to him. He took the hint and did not ask me any questions until we were out of the building. I paused by the letterbox and popped in all but one of the letters Birdie had handed to me, just in case she was looking out of the window.

There was one letter that I kept back. It was a letter from Roberta King to a Miss Georgina King, who must be a sister or an aunt. I would never know because I wasn't in the habit of reading other people's letters. Stealing this one was a necessity, and I was going to give it to Burton as soon as we got into the car.

Peddle brought the car around, and I let out a sigh of relief as soon as I got into the back seat. I opened my purse and pulled out the letter.

"Here's your proof, Detective Chief Inspector," I said, handing it to him. "I hope this establishes Miss King's motive for killing Maria Bocelli."

DCI Burton opened the letter and perused it. Then he pulled out one of the poison pen letters and placed both of them on his lap, side by side. I expected him to smile with joy, but he began to frown instead.

"What is it? What's wrong?" I asked worriedly.

"Look at the two letters, Miss Goring," he replied. "I'm not a handwriting expert, but even I can tell that these two letters weren't written by the same person. Which means Miss King did not write the poison pen letters."

CHAPTER 18

I felt defeated as Springfield let me into Belling House. I was so convinced it was Roberta King who had killed Maria, since she had both motive and opportunity. But I could find no way to connect her to the crime.

DCI Burton had insisted on dropping me off at Bingo's house, telling me to rest for a bit.

"You've been working very hard on this case, Miss Goring. I think you've earned some time off. Meanwhile, I've got to prepare for the inquest, which will take place tomorrow. As I've already informed Lord Belling, he and his mother will need to attend it and give their statements."

When I entered the house, Bingo was in the little parlour, dictating a letter to his secretary.

"I'm sending out Maria's obituary to the press," he said gravely. "The funeral will be three days after the inquest. Her family is arriving from Gloucestershire and will stay at her flat. Basil, please make sure they have everything they need."

"I will, Lord Belling," replied Basil Perkins. "I've made all the arrangements to transport Miss Bocelli's family from the church to Belling House for a funeral tea after the service."

"Thank you, Basil. Get that notice sent out immediately, so it makes tomorrow morning's press," said Bingo. After Basil left the room, he turned to me. "Will you and Jimmy attend the inquest with us, Kitty? I will have to stand up in front of everyone and tell them I have no idea how my fiancée was poisoned right under my nose, even as I sat next to her. And I have a feeling they won't believe me."

"Of course, Bingo. And don't you worry. We will get you out of this mess," I promised. "Although I think it best if we return home after the funeral."

"No! Kitty, you cannot abandon me until this case is solved and my name is cleared. Promise me," he begged, taking both my hands in his.

"All right, Bingo. I won't go anywhere until I clear your name," I said with a sigh, relenting at the panic in his eyes.

Although I did not see what more I could do. We were at a stalemate with the police. Bingo and Sidney Bellamy looked equally guilty in the eyes of the law, but there wasn't any evidence pointing towards either of them.

"There you are," said Jimmy, coming in through one of the French windows, with Scottie and Pudding at his heels. The two little dogs had become fast friends, and it was funny to see Pudding following Scottie around like a little duckling following its mother.

"Have you been for a walk, Scottie?" I asked, as he jumped all over me.

"I'll have you know that I've taken over his training, and he's behaving much better now," crowed Jimmy.

"What about his training to find lost objects? That is much more important than sitting or playing dead," I pointed out.

"I'll just take Pudding upstairs to my mother while the two of you fight over Scottie's training," said Bingo hastily.

When he left the room, Scottie settled in a corner to chew

on a tennis ball, while I brought Jimmy up to date on all that had happened in the past two days.

He let out a low whistle when I told him about the poison pen letters.

"I don't know what to do, Jimmy. Bingo is depending on me to extricate him from this mess, but I don't know how to go about it."

"What did you do when you first began to solve mysteries, Kitty?" he asked.

"I used to make endless lists of suspects, their motives and opportunities," I said, with a laugh.

"Well, then, make one now," he suggested, and I realised that was the best way to clear my mind.

I jumped up and ran to the writing desk by the window.

"I'm sure Bingo won't mind if I borrow some of his writing material," I said, pulling out a sheet of paper and a fountain pen.

I settled down in the chair and began to write my thoughts down.

If there was no way to find who put the poison in both the glasses, we had to find out who had more reason to do so, and from where I stood, there were at least four people who hated Maria enough to want her dead. The first was Bingo, although I didn't really believe he was capable of killing her. The second was Sidney, the third was Roberta King, and the fourth was the person who hated her enough to write those vicious poison pen letters. If only I could find out who it was!

As I was writing, the pen stopped working, and I realised it had run out of ink. There was an inkpot in the writing desk, and it took but a few minutes for me to refill the ink. But when I tried to put the inkpot back in its little cubbyhole, I was met with some resistance. I pulled it out again and felt around the space, and to my surprise, my hand encountered something that was folded and wedged into the back of the cubby hole.

"There's something stuck here," I muttered, and pulled it out with some force. "Hullo, these seem to be some letters."

I went to put them back immediately in a drawer, but one of the letters fell onto the desk, and when I picked it up, I froze in horror. Because it wasn't addressed to anybody living at Belling House.

The letter said, *My darling Maria.*

And it was signed, *Your beloved Sidney.*

CHAPTER 19

"Jimmy, there's a letter here addressed to Maria," I cried. "From Sidney."

"How is that possible?" he asked, jumping up from his chair.

"Maria must have left it here. Do you know, this was exactly what we were looking for when we found the poison pen letters in her house? But what is it doing here?"

"Did you read it?" he asked, and I shook my head immediately.

"Of course not! I can't read someone else's letters!"

"But you were going to do just that if you'd found it in Maria's house, weren't you?" he reasoned.

"Yes, but..."

"Don't think of it as reading something personal to Maria. Think of it as finding evidence that will prove Bingo's innocence, Kitty."

"You're right, Jimmy," I whispered as I opened the letter reluctantly and read its contents. It was exactly as I had predicted. Extremely colourful and frank, it spoke about how much Sidney loved Maria. The letter was dated about a month ago, just around the time that Bingo got engaged to Maria, and in it, Sidney begged her not to leave him. He started with how they had been together through difficult times and were meant to be together forever and ended with dire threats if she went through with the wedding. "This proves Sidney had a bigger motive for killing Maria, especially when you add the scene I witnessed at the party, where he threatened to make her sorry. This might just let Bingo off the hook."

"And what is the other letter?" asked Jimmy.

"Huh?" I asked absently, as I folded the letter and set it down.

"There's another letter with it," insisted Jimmy, pointing to a sheet that had enclosed the original letter.

I opened it, expecting it to be another letter from Sidney to Maria. But it wasn't.

"Jimmy, look at this,' I cried.

Dear Lord Belling,
You have been extremely foolish in your choice of bride. You're about to marry a woman of poor character. Please find enclosed proof of her betrayal.
Yours sincerely,
A good friend

"Another poison pen letter," exclaimed Jimmy.

"Do you realise what this means?" I asked glumly. "It means the needle of suspicion is pointing at Bingo again."

"Why? It points straight at Sidney," argued Jimmy. "Because he wrote that very incriminating letter to Maria."

"But this letter has been opened, which proves that Bingo was aware of Maria's affair with Sidney, and that gives him an even stronger motive if he felt she was making a fool of him."

"Oh no!" cried Jimmy. "The fat is really in the fire this time!"

I rummaged around the drawer until I found the envelope that had enclosed the letters wedged on the other side of the cubby hole. There was no return address or any details about the sender, except a postmark from the Dean Street post office.

I folded both the letters into the envelope and rose from the desk with a sigh.

"I'll telephone DCI Burton and tell him about the new developments," I said wearily.

My head was spinning from all the back and forth. No matter how we moved, we seemed to be going around in circles. And Bingo and Sidney both seemed equally guilty. In theory, at least. Because for the life of me, I could not believe Bingo to be devious enough to keep all this from us and execute such a crime. He simply wasn't clever enough for all that.

"I told you it was Lord Belling, but you wouldn't believe me, Miss Goring," exclaimed PC Peddle when he and Burton walked into the house.

"*What* is Lord Belling?" demanded Bingo, coming out of his study into the hallway, where I was waiting to speak to DCI Burton.

I groaned softly because I had hoped to show the letters to Burton before we spoke to Bingo.

Burton took the letters from my hand and held them out to Bingo.

"Can you explain these letters, Lord Belling?"

Bingo stared at them in comprehension.

"I've never seen them. Who are they from?" he asked in confusion.

I stared at him hard and wondered if that confusion was

real. And try as I might, I couldn't believe it wasn't. Bingo was incapable of such deceit.

"Bingo, one of these is a letter to Maria…from Sidney Bellamy. And the other is an anonymous letter to you, informing you of Maria's relationship with Sidney. His letter was enclosed inside as proof," I said gently.

Burton handed the letters to Bingo, and my friend blanched as he read them.

"I have never seen either of these letters until now. When did they arrive?" he whispered.

"The anonymous letter was delivered five days ago. That means three days before your engagement party," I replied.

"But I didn't get it," insisted Bingo. "And it proves nothing. It's all lies!"

"The envelope was slit open, and the letters have clearly been read, Bingo. You can't deny that," I informed him.

"But…dash it, Kitty! I didn't read either of them!"

"Well, even if you didn't read them, somebody in this house did read them, and it is clear that they did their best to make sure this wedding did not go ahead," said Burton. "As for whether you read the letters, that is an easy thing to find out. We can't test the letters, of course, since you've handled them in front of me. But you haven't touched the envelope so far since Miss Goring found it. If you *had* read the letters, your fingerprints would be all over the envelope, too. Peddle, please send it to have the fingerprints tested."

"Right away, sir," said Peddle, marching away with the envelope held very carefully.

"Right. I'll take these letters into custody, if you please," said Burton, taking the letters back from Bingo. "Lord Belling, I would advise you to consult a solicitor at this point. I will be presenting the letters and the fingerprint analysis at the inquest tomorrow, and if the coroner feels there is enough evidence to bring a charge against you, I must inform you that you will be charged and tried for murder."

CHAPTER 20

As soon as DCI Burton took the letters away, Bingo turned to me and clutched my arm in panic.

"Kitty, I'll be dashed if I hand for a crime I didn't commit! I'll run away tonight!"

"Where will you go, old chap?" asked Jimmy. "There's nowhere to run. If you're innocent, there is nothing anybody can do to you."

"I'll take the next ship to India," babbled Bingo. "No, that's not far enough. I'll have to go to the West Indies. And I'll probably be sick and die on the ship!"

Jimmy grabbed him by the shoulders and shook him hard.

"Snap out of it, old man. You're not going anywhere. Think of the code of the Bellings, Bingo. Your ancestors will turn in their graves if you do anything so cowardly. You will stay here and face the music like a man because you have done nothing wrong. Have you?"

"Yes, Bingo. Think hard, and if you have anything you wish to tell us that might land you in trouble, now is the time to talk about it," I said grimly. "If your fingerprints show up on the envelope, there is no force on earth that will stop DCI Burton from charging you with murder."

"I swear I know nothing about those dashed letters, Kitty. I've never seen them in my life. Not until Burton thrust them at me."

"And if you did know about them, would you have been angry enough to kill Maria?" I asked starkly.

Bingo looked shocked by my blunt question, as did Jimmy, but it had to be asked.

"Kitty, don't you know me at all?" whispered Bingo. "I would never kill anybody. If I had seen those letters earlier, it would have given me the perfect reason to break off the engagement because I would never stand in the way of true love."

"But it wasn't true love on Maria's part, was it? She loved your money more than she loved Sidney," I said sceptically. "And you'd have every right to feel betrayed by that fact."

"Well, I would have felt extremely betrayed if it weren't for the fact that I was having second, third and fourth thoughts about our marriage, and if money was what it took to keep her happy with that blighted Bellamy, I would have considered it a worthy investment," replied Bingo at once.

"You would have paid her not to marry you?" I asked with even more scepticism. "No judge on earth will believe that, Bingo."

"Kitty, I have more money than I know what to do with, but I have only one life. And if I had to put up with a lifetime of my mother and Maria kicking me around like a football, I'd wish for that life to be extremely short," he said with a shudder.

Maybe he was right. Bingo was a coward of epic proportions, and if he had a chance, he would have taken the easiest route out of this marriage, even if it meant having to pay Maria off. And if he had known about her relationship with

Sidney, it would have given him some much-needed leverage.

"Make sure you explain this in great detail to your solicitor," I said crankily.

This case was getting more convoluted than ever. And even with the evidence stacked against him, I found it extremely difficult to believe Bingo could ever pull off such a crime and brazen it out afterwards. Sidney, on the other hand, could brazen it out. As could Roberta King. But now the evidence pointed solidly at somebody in Belling House, because somebody had read those letters and hidden them out of sight.

Why would they do that? The only other reason I could think of was that they wanted the marriage to go ahead, no matter what. And if I were being honest, there wasn't a single person in Belling House who thought Maria Bocelli would have made a good Countess of Belling. Not even the servants.

The better possibility was that somebody in this house had read those letters and realised Bingo was making the biggest mistake of his life, and they had set out to make sure he did not run headlong into danger, as was his wont. They had saved him a lifetime of betrayal and grief. Only they had gone about it the wrong way.

I left Jimmy to help Bingo find a solicitor and took Scottie for a walk in the garden.

Who in Belling House had the largest stake in the matter? Who was the person who would be most affected by Bingo's marriage to Maria? Who had intelligence, cunning and cruelty enough to pull off such a public murder?

The answer to that was wearing a loose gardening smock, and an oversized hat as she ruthlessly pulled out weeds in her rose garden - Letitia, the Dowager Countess of Belling.

CHAPTER 21

"Ah, there you are, Kitty. Have you been *investigating* again? You look slightly haggard," she said, as soon as she saw me.

I wasn't going to say anything until I knew the report of the fingerprint analysis of the envelope. But the uncaring way she was going about her life annoyed me. Her son was about to be charged for a crime he hadn't committed. Why wasn't she more worried? Did she know something I didn't?

"Lady Belling, how far would you have gone to stop this wedding?" I asked bluntly.

She straightened up and glared at me as she held onto her hat.

"I beg your pardon?"

"I know you disliked Maria, but did you actually hate her enough to kill her? You don't seem at all moved by her death."

"Katherine Goring, how dare you speak to me so?" she asked, her bosom swelling with anger as she took in a deep breath. "I have never hidden my dislike of that trollop, so I do not see why I should make a show of false grief at her death. But that does not mean I would ever stoop to murder."

"Lady Belling, Bingo is probably going to be charged for the murder."

"But...why?" she demanded.

"Because we found the letters that somebody in this house had hidden away. The letters that proved Bingo had a much bigger motive for killing Maria than we thought possible."

She turned pale with fear and dropped her gloves absently.

"Who found the letters?"

"I did," I replied, raising my chin and facing her squarely.

"*You?*" she spat, her cheeks flushing with anger. "You are the most meddlesome chit I have ever had the misfortune to meet. We invited you into our house to get Bingo out of this mess, but you've only pushed him deeper into the morass. If my son is arrested for this crime, I will never forgive you until the day I die, or even after, Katherine Goring."

"If your son is arrested for this crime, you have only yourself to blame, Lady Belling," I retorted grimly.

"Me?"

"Yes, you! *You* hid those letters, and *you* killed Maria. It's not too late to save Bingo, Lady Belling. Confess to your crime now!"

"Out!" she shrieked. "Get out of my house now, you insolent girl!"

I drew myself up straight and looked down my nose at her.

"I will go nowhere until I prove Bingo innocent, and if that means I have to prove you murdered your son's fiancée, I will do whatever it takes to do so," I said firmly, before I turned on my heel and walked away, dragging an unwilling Scottie behind me.

"Come on, boy," I murmured. "Let's go find Florence and ask her for a big, juicy bone."

The mention of a bone diverted his attention from chasing butterflies in the rose garden, and Scottie came along willingly.

I stayed in my room for the rest of the day since I wanted to avoid both Bingo and his mother. I worked on teaching Scottie to retrieve hidden objects, but I was beginning to accept that he simply did not have the talent for it. Just before dinner, my mother barged into my bedchamber without so much as a knock.

"What on earth have you been saying to Letitia, you foolish girl?" she demanded wrathfully.

I met her eyes in the mirror calmly and continued to brush my hair.

"I merely told her the truth, Mother. If she does not confess to the crime, she will be responsible for whatever happens to Bingo."

"Kitty, you cannot accuse your hostess of murder," she gasped. "It simply isn't done!"

"But the evidence clearly points to her, Mother," I argued.

"Kitty, I have known Letitia Belling since I was a little girl, and if there is one person on earth you don't want as an enemy, it is her," warned my mother. "She will ruin your reputation in our society."

I gave a rude snort of derision.

"I'd like to see her try. Mother, I will not stand by and allow her to get away with a crime like murder. Especially not when she's willing to sacrifice her son to save her own neck."

"Oh, you simply won't listen to reason! Letitia Belling is not a murderer, you foolish child," cried my mother. "This is what comes of allowing you to dabble in this detective nonsense. You will stop this madness immediately, Katherine, and come home with me tonight. And you will make the most abject apology to Lady Belling."

"I will not," I said roundly. "And what's more, if I find evidence that will convict her, I will make sure Lady Belling is arrested for her crime."

Mother let out a loud sob that almost, but not quite, smote my heart.

"Why am I cursed with two such disobliging children?" she wailed. "Jimmy refuses to come until this case is solved, and now so do you. The two of you will be the ruin of our family!"

"You should be proud of me for bringing murderers to justice, Mother," I said, stung by the fact that my mother simply did not appreciate my talents. Did my only value lie in the fact that I was a beautiful, young aristocrat? And would Mother only appreciate me if I found a rich, aristocratic husband to match?

"There is an entire police force to do that, Kitty."

"Yes, and I solve the crimes that even stump them," I retorted. "Well, you may not care about it, but I am extremely proud of my investigative skills. And what's more, I will never stop solving crimes. After this case is done, I will set up a detective agency and solve crimes for a living. So there!"

Mother staggered and put a hand to her heart.

"You can do whatever you like after I'm dead. Which won't take too long since you're doing your best to drive me into an early grave," she said, with another sob. "I'm going back home tonight with or without you, Kitty. Do as you will."

"Very well, Mother. Ask Henrietta to take good care of you until Jimmy and I return," I said coldly.

"I might be dead by the time you return, but why would you care?"

After that last shot, my mother waddled angrily out of my

bedchamber, and I slumped against the frame of the four-poster bed. My maid, Florence, who had been a silent observer all this while, maintained a disapproving silence until I could stand it no longer.

"I must do this, Florence. I cannot allow an innocent man to hang for a crime he did not commit."

"I don't think the police would ever find evidence to prove Lord Belling had the brains to pull this off, miss. He won't hang for nothin'. They will probably keep him in jail for a bit and then let him go. And that would only knock some sense into his thick head. Marrying an opera singer, indeed. What *was* he thinking?"

Florence was an even bigger snob than my mother and Lady Belling put together.

I decided not to argue with her but get on with what I needed to do. The first thing I needed to do was go down to dinner and put up a brave face because I wasn't going to give Lady Belling the satisfaction of thinking she had intimidated me in any way. The second thing I needed to do was to figure out how she might have committed the crime, if indeed, she had done it.

CHAPTER 22

I met Prudence Sharp, Lady Belling's companion, on the stairs, and we walked downstairs together.

"Is it true, Miss Goring? That they might arrest Lord Belling for Miss Bocelli's murder?"

She looked terrified, like a frightened rabbit, and no wonder, for a life spent running after Lady Belling could not have been easy. But if there was anybody who knew everything about Letitia Belling, it was her.

"Maybe," I said politely.

"Lady Belling is furious that you found the letters and gave them to the police," she confided, with a quick look around to confirm her employer wasn't in earshot.

I decided to cast my hook into the water.

"She should have shown the letters to Bingo while she still had the chance," I murmured, and Prudence froze for a moment.

"What is it?" I asked immediately, but she shook her head.

"I...I...don't know what you mean, Miss Goring."

"Come now, Prudence. You know as well as I do that Lady Belling was the one who read those letters. But how did that come about? Was she in the habit of reading her son's private correspondence?"

Prudence looked as if she was willing to take a flying leap over the banister to get away from me, but there was nowhere she could go.

"I…I…Lady Belling is a very loving mother, even if she's very strict," she whispered.

"How far is she willing to take that strictness, Prudence? You haven't answered my question. Is she in the habit of opening her son's letters?"

"No! That is…I suppose she only did it because he didn't believe what was in the previous one," she stammered.

"The previous what?" I asked sharply, and Prudence gasped as she backed away from me.

"I'm sorry, Miss Goring. I've said too much. She'll never forgive me if she finds out," she cried, as she ran back up the stairs.

Drat the girl! What did she mean by the previous one? Was there another letter before this? And if so, why did Bingo not tell me that?

I ran down the stairs furiously. Benjamin Belling had a lot to answer for, I decided, as I banged on the door to his study.

"You louse," I cried when I entered, and both Bingo and Jimmy jumped to their feet. "You absolute lying louse!"

"Kitty! What's wrong?" asked Jimmy, laying down his whiskey and soda, and approaching me cautiously, while Bingo stayed frozen in place.

I pointed at Bingo with a shaking finger and tried to control my anger.

"Did you know your best friend has been lying to us? He said he didn't know anything about Maria's relationship with Sidney, but that's not possible because apparently, there was another letter before the one I found in the writing desk."

"How the deuce do you know that?" demanded Bingo angrily.

"Aha!" I cried. "So, you do admit it?"

"Dash it, Kitty! It was just one of those poison pen letters saying nasty things about Maria. One doesn't believe such tripe. One burns them, that's all."

"If that is true, why didn't you mention it earlier, Bingo?" I asked, crossing my arms over my chest.

"Because it had nothing to do with anything."

"Really? Or was it because you failed to heed your mother's warnings about Maria after she read the first letter, and you know at some level that the second one might have driven her to murder?"

Bingo blanched at my words, and I thought he was about to faint.

"Bingo," cried Jimmy. "Sit down, old chap. Take a deep breath. Pour him a brandy, Kitty. Can't you see the chap's just had a big shock?"

I poured him a glass of brandy that he downed in one big gulp, and some colour returned to Bingo's face.

"What did you say about Mother?" he stammered.

"Somebody in this house read those letters, Bingo," I said gently, my anger starting to drain. "Who would dare to read Lord Belling's private correspondence, except his mother?"

"But if she did read them, why didn't she tell me?" he asked plaintively.

"Because you didn't heed her the first time. Maybe she decided to take care of the problem on her own."

"That's absurd! What you're suggesting is…is…simply ridiculous, Kitty. My mother is not a murderer!"

Just then, we heard the second dinner gong, and Bingo leapt out of his chair.

"It's time to go into the dining room, Kitty. We will

discuss this later. Please don't mention it in front of my mother."

"I'm afraid…it might be too late for that advice," I said, with a sheepish look, and Bingo and Jimmy groaned in unison.

"Please don't tell me you accused my mother of murder," whimpered Bingo.

"If we're poisoned at dinner tonight, Kitty, I will blame you forever," said Jimmy severely. "You cannot accuse your hostess of murder. Not only is it the height of ill manners, but it's also plain stupid. Anyone with half a brain would have told you so."

"She will never forgive you for this, Kitty," groaned Bingo. "And I'll never hear the end of it. Ugh!"

I followed him out of the study feeling slightly contrite. Bingo might be an idiot, but he did not deserve to suffer for it for the rest of his life.

The atmosphere during dinner was particularly icy. Luckily, I was sitting at the other end of the table from Lady Belling, with many people and a huge flower arrangement obscuring my view of her angry face that looked as if it had permanent lines drawn in it by her fury.

During dinner, I noticed the first footman, Miller, and I remembered our conversation when he denied serving the ill-fated table that night. Which brought me to the most pressing question on my mind.

That night, Bingo was sitting between Maria and Lady Belling. How could she have dropped cyanide into two glasses that were in front of Maria without being noticed? As far as I knew, she hadn't risen from her seat to go over to Maria's side. And if she had leaned over to do it, Bingo would surely have noticed it. As would Maria.

So, how did she do it? All I could think of was that she

had an accomplice that night. And the only person who came to mind was the footman, Miller.

I studied him covertly during dinner and wondered if I could find a way to question him further. But if he had maintained his statement when DCI Burton questioned him, what chance did I have of breaking him down?

As we walked out of the dining room, Jimmy pinched the inside of my elbow.

"Why were you staring at that footman as if you were worried he was about to poison your soup? Did you see him do something?" he whispered anxiously.

I led him closer to the window, so we wouldn't be overheard.

"No, but I think he might have poisoned Maria on Lady Belling's orders," I whispered back.

Jimmy's brows furrowed in confusion.

"John?" he asked.

"Miller," I corrected.

"Who?"

"The first footman's real name is Rodney Miller. Lady Belling can't be bothered to remember it, so she calls him John. But we don't have to go along with that asinine habit because names matter, Jimmy. You wouldn't like it if she took to calling you Johnny, would you?"

"I'd be happy if she never called me again for the rest of my life," he muttered, running a finger along the inside of his collar. "That woman terrifies me, Kitty. More so now that I know you suspect her to be capable of murder."

"Oh, I'll protect you from the big, bad witch, brother dear," I said, with a grin.

"Hmph! Now tell me why you suspect poor Molar."

"Miller," I snapped, and he grinned back.

"Gotcha!"

"Idiot," I said fondly. "Look, Lady Belling can't have

poisoned Maria by herself because Bingo would have noticed her leaning across the table to drop something in both glasses. She needed a stooge, and who could be more convenient than her own footman?"

Jimmy frowned in response.

"Yes, but as far as I remember, that fellow was hovering around my side of the room during the dance display. I know this because he lent me a match when I ran out of matches for my cigarette."

I stared at him in disbelief.

"What? That can't be possible, Jimmy. If I remember correctly, you were standing by the far wall."

"As was Miller," he insisted. "At one point, he stated to go across the room, but then, changed his mind for some reason and came back to his original spot. I remember it clearly because it was dashed odd."

I knew what he was saying. The best-trained servants moved in invisible circles around you at parties, never intruding on your consciousness, and when they did something that brought them to your notice, you tended to remember that.

"But if it wasn't him, then who was it?" I wondered aloud.

I remembered what Miller had said to DCI Burton. There was another footman that night. Someone who wasn't part of Bingo's staff.

"Jimmy, would you notice it if you saw a footman who wasn't wearing the same livery as the others?"

"Of course," said my brother. "That's the kind of thing you'd notice without meaning to, if you know what I mean."

"I do know what you mean. And that means I really need to speak with Miller."

We went back into the dining room where the footmen and maids were clearing the table. Jimmy beckoned to

Miller, and after a scared glance at Springfield, who nodded his permission, Miller came towards us.

"Yes, sir?" he asked, his throat working nervously.

"Relax, old chap. We just want to ask you a few questions. Er…go on, Kitty."

"I'm sorry to take you away from your work, Miller," I said with a warm smile. "I hope we didn't get you in trouble with Springfield."

Miller relaxed enough to smile at us shyly.

"Not at all, miss. How can I help you?"

"You mentioned earlier that there was another footman serving Lord Belling's table on the night of the party. Was he wearing the same livery as you?"

"Indeed, miss. And I suspect he stole it from my room," replied Miller indignantly. "It is still missing, and Mr Springfield insists he will have to cut the cost of the livery from my wages since we're only given two at a time."

"I'm very sorry to hear that, Miller," I said, and shot a meaningful glance at Jimmy, who luckily took the hint.

He immediately pulled out a tenner from his pocket and slipped it into Miller's hand.

"Here's something for the trouble, old chap."

"Why, thank you, sir," said Miller in surprise. "You didn't have to…"

"Oh, don't worry about it. Now, did you see this livery-stealing fellow again?" asked Jimmy.

"No, sir. If I had, I would have got me livery back. And a fair disgrace to it, he was," confided Miller. "I didn't see him up close, but me livery was hanging off him like it was four sizes too big. And he wore a hat. Inside the house! You're not allowed to wear a hat during table service, are you?"

We thanked Miller and walked back into the hallway.

"Do you know what this means, Jimmy?" I asked excitedly. "It means we now know that someone pretended to be a footman to poison Maria Bocelli. Whether they did it of their own accord or at Lady Belling's bidding remains to be seen."

Jimmy groaned and rubbed his face wearily.

"I dunno how you do this all the time, Kitty. I'm ready to drop into bed," he said with a big yawn.

"Go on. I'll take Scottie for one quick walk around the garden to clear my head," I said, whistling for my dog.

He came bounding up to me, and I put on my coat before I tied his leash onto his collar. The garden was very peaceful in the dark, and the sound of the crickets made me pleasantly drowsy. We were passing the herb garden when Scottie bounded off to chase a mouse.

I decided to let him play for a few minutes before I took him back in and stood under the overhang of the terrace on the first floor. After five minutes, I got bored of waiting and stepped forward to call out to Jimmy. As soon as I moved from the spot, I heard a loud crash behind me and turned around in horror to see a large flowerpot lying in smithereens exactly where I had been standing. It was one of the massive flowerpots lining the edge of the terrace above.

I looked up immediately and got the feeling somebody had just moved back into the cover of darkness on the terrace above me. My heart was racing, and I kept getting distracted by the fact that if I hadn't moved when I did, I could have been killed by the flowerpot crashing onto my head. And it hadn't fallen on its own. Somebody had lobbed it at my head!

I left Scottie in the garden and slipped into the house through the side door that I had left open, and raced up the stairs to the terrace to see if my assailant was still there. When I arrived huffing and puffing to the terrace, I saw all my fears had come true.

There, leaning against the balustrade, peering out over the edge, was the stately figure of Lady Belling.

CHAPTER 23

My first instinct was to confront her. How dare she make such a blatant attempt on my life? But better sense prevailed, and I tiptoed downstairs as quietly as I could.

Lady Belling was getting desperate now, and who knew what she could do when provoked? I had no intention of confronting her alone. It was much better to do it with DCI Burton by my side.

I went to the door and gave a low whistle to call Scottie, and to my relief, he came to me immediately. I gathered him up and ran to my bedroom, not feeling safe until I had locked the door and set a chair under the door handle.

It was still some time before I stopped shaking. I spent a restless night, tossing and turning in bed until Florence rattled the door handle. I let her in cautiously, and she took one look at my haggard face and pursed her lips in displeasure.

"That's it, miss. We're packing our bags and going home. This place is giving you nightmares," she declared as she poured my tea.

I sighed heavily because running away was not an option. I refused to give that old hag the satisfaction of driving me away. I was going to battle her on her own ground, and I was going to defeat her.

"I'm not going down for breakfast, Florence. I'll have it in my room. And can you ask Sir James to come up to my room after I finish my tea?"

When Florence went out to summon Jimmy, I splashed some cold water on my face and stared at the shadows under my eyes in horror. Who was this frightened creature? Anger sparked through me at the thought of allowing Lady Belling to cow me to this extent.

There was a soft tap on my door, and Jimmy poked his head into the room.

"What's wrong, Kitty? Florence said you look like you've seen a ghost, and she's not wrong," he exclaimed. "What happened to you?"

"Lady Belling tried to kill me last night, that's what happened," I said waspishly.

Jimmy's jaw dropped at my revelation.

"What did she do? And are you all right?"

"I am, thank you. She chucked a flowerpot at my head while I was walking Scottie, and it narrowly missed hitting me," I explained.

"How did you know it was her?"

"I looked up immediately and saw someone move back from the edge of the terrace, but it was too dark to tell who it was. So, I ran upstairs and found Lady Belling peering over the edge of the terrace."

"Did you confront the old bat?" he asked indignantly.

"For once in my life, I did the sensible thing and flew into my room and barricaded the door," I said, with a watery laugh.

"Good job, old thing. What do we do next?"

"We call Scotland Yard," I said grimly. "And by that, I mean I stay barricaded in here, and you go downstairs to call DCI Burton. Tell him it's urgent."

Jimmy flew downstairs to call Burton, and I stood staring out of the window until he returned, my breakfast lying forgotten on my bed.

To his credit, DCI Burton arrived within thirty minutes, and when I went downstairs to speak to him in the little parlour, he looked worried. Unfortunately, that worry turned to fury as I narrated my tale, and as it turned out, that fury was directed against me.

"You little fool! You could have been killed," he snarled. "Why did you have to confront her at all? I told you not to do anything until we got the fingerprint analysis."

"I did what I felt was best. And I am glad I did, Detective Chief Inspector, for I found out a lot more than you did. Apparently, this wasn't the first letter Bingo received. He burnt the first one because he thought it was just a poison pen letter. And it was Lady Belling who opened the letter that I found. She probably hid it from Bingo because she wanted to take care of it herself."

As soon as I finished talking, a quick glance at DCI Burton's stony countenance told me that rubbing his nose in my success was probably not the best idea. He seemed to have taken it really badly.

"Thank you for your help with this case, Miss Goring. But I think you've overstayed your welcome at Belling House. It is time you returned home while you still can. I wouldn't put it past Lady Belling to make another attempt on your life," he said stiffly.

I crossed my arms over my chest and raised my chin defiantly.

"I'm not going anywhere, Detective Chief Inspector. I promised Bingo I wouldn't let him hang for a crime he didn't commit, and I'm going to keep my word. Besides, I cannot allow Lady Belling to think she succeeded in frightening me away," I said lightly, but his stony countenance did not budge.

"In that case, Miss Goring, I am very sorry to tell you, but your involvement in this case is over. If you lift one little finger to do anything more, I will arrest you for obstruction of justice."

My jaw dropped in stupefaction and anger.

"Of all the nasty, ungrateful men I have ever met, you are the worst, Detective Chief Inspector," I hissed. "The *worst*!"

"I am sorry you feel that way, Miss Goring," he growled. "But if I have to lock you up to keep you safe, then that is exactly what I will do."

Someone cleared their throat, and Burton and I turned around to see Jimmy rolling his eyes at us.

"If the two of you are done squabbling like school-children, can I make a suggestion? Burton, you cannot cut my sister out of this adventure. Not after she's almost helped you crack the case. That is beneath you, old chap. And Kitty, he is right. You cannot go careening headfirst into danger like you normally do. So, here's what we're going to do. *I* will keep you safe," he announced, and paused for effect.

"You?" Burton and I asked in unison, and the disbelief in our voices made my brother furious.

"Now, who's being ungrateful?" he demanded.

I blew out a heavy breath and gave him an apologetic smile.

"I'm sorry, Jimmy. That was very rude of me. Unlike some people…"

Here I paused to shoot a sweet smile at Burton, enjoying the way a muscle pulsed at the corner of his jaw as he glared at me.

"Unlike some people, I am very grateful for the help I receive. But you know you would be less than helpless in a crisis. You're as bad as Bingo, which is why you're the best of friends."

Jimmy let out a snort of disgust.

"I'm much better in a crisis than that toerag, thank you very much," he muttered.

"I think we will all feel better if I take charge of keeping Miss Goring safe," declared Burton.

"Not if you're going to keep me locked in my room," I argued, and he looked upwards as if he were begging for patience from the Lord.

"Fine, but if I'm not around, you have to promise to stay in your room. No wandering around the garden alone at night," he ordered, and I nodded my head meekly. "Now, there has been one more development in the case."

"What is that?" I asked in surprise.

"I matched the handwriting on that letter against the two samples that we have, and it matched that of Miss Roberta King."

"Miss King tried to break up Bingo's engagement. But why?"

"She says it was jealousy and anger. She was supposed to take Miss Bocelli's place in the opera, but since she refused to step down even after she became the Countess of Belling, Miss King decided to get her own back by sowing mistrust in their relationship. So you see, she had motive, opportunity, and she acted against Maria Bocelli even before the party. Until you told me of the attempt on your life, I was convinced I had enough to charge her with murder.

"And now?"

"Now, I'm more inclined to believe your theory. I think it is time we had a word with Lady Belling."

CHAPTER 24

Together, we marched upstairs to Lady Belling's sitting room. Prudence gaped at us in surprise when she opened the door. I spotted my mother ensconced in a wingback chair by the fire with a teacup and plate of crumpets, and I had to admit I was hurt that she was socialising with the woman who tried to kill her daughter.

Then I remembered that my mother didn't know Lady Belling had tried to kill me last night.

"What is it, Detective Chief Inspector? I thought the inquest wasn't until later this afternoon," complained Lady Belling.

"It isn't, Your Ladyship. I'm here to investigate a complaint made by Miss Goring. She alleges that you made an attempt on her life last night."

"She *what*?" asked Lady Belling, dropping her teacup in shock.

"Kitty, are you mad?" cried my mother, setting down her cup before she spilled tea all over herself.

"No, Mother. I'm not mad," I said quietly. "I was walking

Scottie last night when a large flowerpot almost crashed on my head under the terrace outside Lady Belling's room. I saw someone on the terrace, but it was too dark to see their face, so I raced upstairs to see who it was, and I caught Lady Belling peering over the edge of the balcony."

"It wasn't me, Detective Chief Inspector," wailed Lady Belling. "I am being framed for something I did not do!"

"I saw you with my own eyes," I spat, and she nodded.

"I agree that I did go outside when I heard the crash. But I wasn't the one who threw that thing at your head. And I can prove it. I wasn't alone when I heard the crash."

"Oh, and who was with you?" I asked with a sneer. "Was it Prudence?"

"No, it was me," exclaimed my mother furiously. "Letitia and I were enjoying a nightcap together when we heard the crash, and she went out to investigate what had happened."

I stared at her in dismay, because if it had been Prudence, I could easily have believed that Lady Belling had bullied her into taking her side. But my mother was another matter altogether. I couldn't doubt my mother's claim. Why would she side with the woman who tried to kill her daughter?

"I…I beg your pardon?"

"That's right, Kitty. Letitia did not try to kill you, nor did she kill that blighted woman, Maria Bocelli. You must stop this madness," she begged.

"I'm sorry, Lady Belling," I said stiffly.

"That is quite all right, but please leave my room immediately," she replied with hauteur. "I am not accustomed to being treated with such disrespect in my own house."

DCI Burton apologised for the intrusion, and we left the room, feeling slightly foolish.

"I can't believe it," I said slowly. "How is it possible? It can't be anyone else."

"Unless Lady Belling has an accomplice in the house," replied Burton, as we went downstairs.

"The footman, Kitty! Why do we keep forgetting the blasted footman?" demanded Jimmy.

"I didn't forget about him. I was just distracted by what happened last night," I said sheepishly.

I quickly filled Burton in on the developments on that front, and he frowned when he heard about the footman wearing a hat at table service.

"That's absurd. Why would he do that?" he asked.

"Because he didn't know any better," guessed Jimmy. "He wasn't a professional footman, after all."

"You don't have to be a footman to know they don't wear hats inside the house," replied Burton dryly.

"Can we forget about the hat for now, and think about who it could be? And if he tried to kill me last night? And how do we tie Lady Belling to the case? You will need much more evidence against her if you hope to make the charges against her stick."

"We have to trace the poison, Miss Goring. If we can connect Lady Belling to the poison, we can connect her to the murder. Now, the only places she could have got the cyanide are the garden or the pharmacy.

"Jimmy, can you go to the pharmacy with PC Peddle and check if they delivered any cyanide to Belling House?" I asked.

"Meanwhile, shall we speak to the gardener?" asked Burton.

It wasn't easy to spot old Tom, the gardener, in the gardens of Belling House. He liked to blend in with the trees. Tom was a wizened, grizzled old man who had looked like he was ninety even when I first met him as a little girl, and he hadn't changed a bit now.

"Tom, could we speak to you for a minute, please?" I

asked, and crossed my fingers behind my back, hoping he was in a good mood today.

His mood was exactly like the weather, sunny when the sun was shining and miserable on wet days that aggravated his rheumatism.

"Aye," he grunted. "I've nothing much to do all day anyway. These young 'uns do all the work now. They don't need an old timer telling them what to do."

I steered him away from his grouses against the two under-gardeners and led him towards the shed.

"Well, I was wondering…do you still use cyanide to get rid of wasps in here?"

"'Course, we do! Nothing like it, I always says!"

"And where do you store it?"

"In the little shed, where else?" he asked, frowning at me from under beetled brows. It took me right back to my childhood when he used to tell us off for stealing his apples before they were quite ready.

"Can you show us, please?" I begged.

"Planning to poison yer young man here?" he asked, with a wicked cackle as he hobbled over to the little shed.

"I'm quaking in my boots," said DCI Burton, enjoying my discomfiture.

"He's not my young man," I said clearly. "We are colleagues."

"Not for want of trying, I bet," said old Tom, and I frowned at him repressively.

I didn't remember him being quite so chatty when I was younger. But in his dotage, he seemed to have turned into a proper Cupid. All he needed were a pair of wings, a nappy and a bow and arrow, I thought, avoiding Henry Burton's gaze completely.

He took his sweet time unlocking the door and finally allowed us to step into the dark, cool interiors of the shed.

He pointed to a bottle on the shelf marked Poison - Cyanide.

"That's the one," he said, and then frowned mightily as he squinted at the bottle. "Here! What's this? This bottle was brand new and sealed. Why is it almost empty?"

I gave Burton a triumphant glance, and he reached forward to grab the bottle gingerly with his snowy white handkerchief.

"I'll take that, if you don't mind," he said, and Tom gave him a shrewd look.

"Copper, are ya? Going to find the one that did the master's lady in?"

"I will try my best," replied Burton.

"*We* will try our best," I added firmly, and Tom turned to scowl at me.

"A murder case is no place for a woman. This one's always been looking for trouble, even when she was a little girl. You'll have your hands full with her," he said to Burton over my head, as if I weren't even there.

I took a deep breath and swallowed the sharp retort that leapt to my tongue before I turned to Tom with a question.

"Who else has a key to the shed?"

"Only the grand old lady. She don't let anyone else near the poison. Says it's got ter be under lock and key."

"And how often does she give her key to someone to take things from this shed?"

"Never," he replied promptly. "This here is my domain, and I don't let anybody mess with it, especially with Tweedle Dee and Tweedle Dum out there."

He was referring to the two under-gardeners, with whom he clearly did not get along.

"And you're sure you did not lend the key to anyone?" asked Burton.

"No, sir. Only I controls the poison around here. Don't

want those dum-dums poisoning my pretty rose beds, now, do I?"

When I met Burton's eyes, I knew what he was thinking. Lady Belling was the only person apart from Tom who had access to the poison. The motive and opportunity were already there. We just had to build the evidence against her one by one.

CHAPTER 25

I smiled at Tom and dropped a soft kiss on his wizened cheek.

"Take care, dear Tom, and thank you for your help."

"Go on with yer," he said gruffly, flushing bright red as he turned to lock the shed again.

Burton and I walked back to the house, and I realised I was close to tears.

"What's the matter, Miss Goring?"

"I feel really bad for poor Bingo. He will be devastated when he hears that his mother killed his fiancée. Do you think they will hang her?"

"I highly doubt it. They would probably institutionalise her for the rest of her life. But let's take one step at a time, Miss Goring," he said gently. "Let us first check for fingerprints on the bottle. Whether it was Lady Belling who dropped the poison into the drinks, or she got an accomplice to do it, they might have left some prints. I hope they shed some light on our murderer."

"Who could the accomplice be? Do you think it could be one of the footmen?"

"Maybe. Or it could also be someone completely beholden to Lady Belling in some way. Can you think of somebody like that?" Burton asked.

"Basil Perkins," I said immediately. "His father was the vicar at the local parish. Bingo's father took Basil under his care and paid for his education - a fact that Lady Belling never lets him forget. That's why he works as Bingo's secretary, instead of as an attaché to an ambassador. Basil is very talented, but Lady Belling has never allowed him to fly. Maybe she promised him his freedom in exchange for this favour?"

"Is that the man with the tortoiseshell glasses?" asked Burton.

I nodded in reply.

"I didn't see him during the dance display until after the murder. It wouldn't have been very difficult for him to put on the footman's livery, pretend to serve drinks, and then change back into his normal clothes quickly. It could also explain why he fumbled the tray. Basil is practically blind without his glasses."

Scottie came running to greet us when we walked up to the house. Rather, he came running to greet DCI Burton, who was his old friend. He squirmed in ecstasy when Burton rubbed his ears and called him a good boy.

"Yes, he's a very good boy, but he's also a dum-dum. Just like Tom's under-gardeners," I said with an eye roll. "I've been trying so hard to teach him to find lost objects, but all he likes to do is chase mice and anything that looks like a ball."

DCI Burton disappeared to make some telephone calls to the Yard regarding the bottle of poison, and I went into the little parlour to await him. When I entered, Prudence was wandering around the room like a lost lamb, wringing her hands in distress.

"What's the matter, Prudence?"

"Oh, miss. Lady Belling dictated a list of guests to be invited to the funeral reception, and I've misplaced it already. She will have my hide if she finds out," she cried.

"Where did you leave your notebook last?"

"It was on a sheet of paper, and I'm pretty sure I left it in this room. And I'm afraid it's gone forever. Sir James was making balls out of paper for Scottie and Pudding to play with, and I have a feeling he might have used it for that purpose."

"Oh no! Those little beasts don't spare any ball, and one made of paper stands no chance against their sharp teeth. I'm afraid you will have to beg Lady Belling to help you make another one."

"Oh, dear. She's in a bit of a mood," she said, with a shudder. "But it will be worse if I don't own up to it right away."

"Good luck," I said, with a grin.

I didn't envy Prudence her life at all. She was one of Lady Belling's poor relations, and a distant one at that, and in exchange for a roof over her head and food in her belly, she was forced into a life of eternal drudgery. Just like Basil Perkins.

DCI Burton came in just then, and a thought struck me.

"Detective Chief Inspector, will you be interrogating Basil and checking his fingerprints against those on the bottle before the inquest?"

"Yes, Miss Goring, and also against the remnants of the flowerpot that almost killed you last night. The fingerprints team is arriving within a few minutes. I beg your pardon, but why is your dog trying to eat the sofa?" he asked in surprise.

"Scottie, what on earth are you doing there?" I yelped. "He's trying to squeeze himself under the sofa."

"Maybe he sees a mouse," said Burton, with a grin.

"Or a ball," I replied, with a laugh. "Move over, you beast. Let me have a look."

"Allow me, Miss Goring," said DCI Burton.

I caught Scottie by the collar and kept him out of Burton's way as he reached his long hand under the sofa and came out with a few balls of paper.

"I told you he was after a ball," I said, laughing, when a thought struck me.

"Oh, please do check if one of those balls is a guest list belonging to Lady Belling's companion. She's misplaced the one for the funeral reception, and Lady Belling will be very cross with her if she has to help her make another one."

Burton very kindly unrolled the balls and gave them a quick once-over before he rolled them up again and threw them around the room for Scottie to chase.

"Here you go, Miss Goring," he said when he found the guest list, holding out a crumpled sheet of paper.

I extended my hand to take it from him, but he suddenly froze with his hand suspended mid-air, and then slowly reeled it back in to stare at the sheet of paper. Then he reached into his coat pocket and pulled out another one.

He placed them side by side and beckoned me closer. On one side was the guest list for Maria's funeral reception, and on the other…I gasped in horror as I recognised one of the poison pen letters I had found in Maria's flat.

They were both written in the same hand.

I sank onto my haunches and stared at DCI Burton.

"Prudence wrote those letters! Is that really possible?"

"Anything is possible, Miss Goring," he replied grimly.

"We need to confront her at once."

"Wait, Miss Goring. I will have her fingerprints matched against the bottle of poison and the remnants of the flower-pot, from both the letters. The sooner we have all the evidence in place, the better it will be. I will telephone the Yard and ask them to have the inquest delayed by a few days, so we can build an airtight case right from the start. Don't confront Miss Sharp until the report of the fingerprint analysis comes in."

"Do you think it likely that the poison pen letters were unconnected to the murder?"

"It does not seem likely, Miss Goring. It is far more likely that Lady Belling's companion was her accomplice in the murder."

"Wait! I know for a fact that she was sitting with Henrietta Alton, my mother's companion, at a table at the back of the ballroom."

"Can that be verified by Miss Alton?"

"I can call her in right now," I suggested.

When he nodded, I rang the bell and asked the butler to summon Henrietta.

She came in looking surprised to see DCI Burton.

"Good morning, Miss Goring...Detective Chief Inspector. How may I be of assistance?"

"Henrietta..." I began, but DCI Burton cut me off.

"Where were you on the night of the murder, Miss Alton? Between half past eight and nine o'clock?"

"I was sitting at the table that I was assigned to, Detective Chief Inspector. It was at the far end of the ballroom," she replied promptly.

"Is there anyone who can verify that, Miss Alton?"

She flushed a little, and I wondered why.

"Mr Basil Perkins spent most of the evening sitting with me."

"And apart from Mr Perkins, can anyone else verify that? This is a matter of great importance, Miss Alton," he said sternly, making it sound as if it was her we suspected.

"Prudence Sharp was sitting with us earlier, but…well…I suppose I must let you know that Mr Basil Perkins and I are walking out together, as it were. And Prudence left us alone at the table before the dance display to give us some privacy. She retired to her room because she had a bit of a headache from all the noise."

"Thank you for your help, Miss Alton," said Burton with a kind smile.

Henrietta turned to me worriedly, and I let out a loud squeal of delight.

"Basil Perkins is a wonderful man, my dear. I'm very happy for you."

"Thank you, Miss Goring. I haven't told your mother yet…"

"My lips are sealed," I promised hastily.

She left the room in a cloud of joy, and I turned to glare at Burton.

"Why did you make it sound as if you were interrogating Henrietta?" I asked.

"Because when she goes out of that room, Miss Sharp will most probably ask her why she was called in. This way, she can tell her that it was she, Henrietta, who was under suspicion, and not Miss Sharp."

"So, this rules Basil Perkins out completely," I mused. "Henrietta would never lie. If she says Basil was with her for most of the evening, I would believe it. And Prudence retired to her room before the dance display."

"Yes, which gives opportunity as far as the murder is concerned. But we don't know her motive yet. We know she sent hateful letters to Miss Bocelli. But did she do that of her own accord, or on Lady Belling's behalf?"

"And what about the footman? Where does he come in?" I asked glumly. "It still doesn't make sense."

"It will make sense once we have the fingerprint reports, Miss Goring. Don't worry about it. Get some rest tonight, and please don't go wandering around the gardens," he said sternly, before he went to organise the fingerprinting of the flowerpot.

CHAPTER 26

As I was getting ready to go down for dinner that night, a sudden thought struck me, and I turned to Florence with a groan.

"I don't feel very well, Florence. I feel a headache coming on. Please tell my mother that I would like to go to bed right away," I said, rubbing my temples and trying to look unwell.

Florence did not look very convinced, but she didn't argue with me.

"Should I bring you some dinner on a tray, miss?" was all she asked.

"No! I feel too queasy to eat, I'm afraid. I'll just change into my nightgown and go to bed immediately. Be a dear and tell my mother I mustn't be disturbed, will you?"

"I will, miss. First, let me help you get changed out of these clothes," she said, shooting me an odd glance.

"No, thank you. I can do it by myself. I really want to be alone, Florence," I said crossly, and she finally agreed to leave me alone.

When she was gone, I locked my door from the inside

and waited until I heard footsteps going downstairs for dinner, one by one. When there were no more footsteps heard, I waited for ten more minutes before I silently unlocked my door and poked my head into the corridor.

I could hear a murmur of voices coming from the dining room, which meant that the dinner service had started. I gave it five more minutes before I ventured out of my room and tiptoed my way across the long corridor to the family wing.

I knew Prudence's room was right next to Lady Belling's, and I knocked softly on the door just to be safe, and when there was no response, I gently tried the doorknob.

To my relief, it opened, and I slipped into the room and shut the door behind me. I made straight for her small wooden wardrobe and began to rummage through it. I knew I was playing a dangerous game, and if she saw me in her room, I'd have no answer for her. But I had to try my luck since this was the only explanation!

It wasn't in her wardrobe, nor was it in the small chest of drawers next to it. Out of desperation, I bent down and peeked under the bed. I could see something stuffed into the farthest corner. It was a packet of some kind.

I stretched my arm and reached under the bed to grab it by the edge and pull it out slowly. When it was out, I stood up and dusted myself off before I laid the packet on the bed and tore open the newspaper sheets it was wrapped in.

And there it was…*the footman's uniform, complete with hat.*

Proof that Prudence Sharp had masqueraded as a footman to poison Maria Bocelli. I folded the uniform neatly and wrapped it in the newspaper all over again before I bent down and pushed it back into place. I had what I needed. Now all I had to do was telephone DCI Burton at the Yard, and he would do the needful.

When I straightened up, my eyes went to the door that was right across from me, and I froze.

Prudence stood in the doorway, staring at me with a curious light in her eyes.

CHAPTER 27

"I...I.." I began to stammer, wondering how I could explain my presence in her room.

She came in and shut the door, wandering over to stand next to me.

"You really shouldn't have come here, Miss Goring," she said softly.

"I'm sorry. I'll just show myself out now," I said, trying to walk past her, but she blocked my way.

"You know, don't you? I don't know how you guessed it, but you know."

"I don't know what you're talking about," I whispered, and she smiled.

A cold smile that struck fear into my heart.

She leaned forward suddenly, and I tried not to flinch in response.

"You know what I've been up to, don't you?"

I stared at her in horror, wondering if I had ever truly looked at her, and if I had, how had I missed the glint of madness in her eyes? I had never looked past her frumpy exterior, frizzy hair, thick spectacles and air of total inefficiency. Or had that all been an act?

Because this Prudence was very confident, cocky even. She stood up straighter and looked straight into your eyes, her own glinting with anger and hate. Before I could respond, she reached into her bodice and pulled out a tiny snub-nosed revolver that she pointed at me.

"Where did you get that?" I asked in horror.

"It belongs to Lady Belling. I borrowed it, just as I borrowed the key to the potting shed," she replied quite cheerfully.

"And what do you intend to do with it, Prudence?" I asked tartly. "You can hardly shoot me inside a house full of people and expect to get away with it. Don't risk your future and your life for Lady Belling's sake."

She gave a little surprised laugh when she heard that.

"Oh no! Do you really think I'm doing this on *her* behalf? Oh, my dear Miss Goring. You're not half as smart as you like to believe."

"And if you want me to believe *you* are smart enough to pull off such an audacious crime, you must be out of your tiny little mind," I retorted in the same tone.

I had a feeling it was in my best interests not to show my fear of her madness. Because what else could it be that had forced Prudence to go to such lengths to kill Maria? And was it all her own doing? But why?

"Shut *up*," she hissed, waving her gun in my direction.

Again, it took all my strength not to flinch, but I did it somehow.

"You're not stupid enough to shoot me, Prudence. The others would arrive before your gun stopped smoking. You don't have a prayer of getting out without being nabbed if you shoot me. So, I'm going to leave your bedroom now, and you can save all your theatricals for the police," I said firmly, turning to go around her.

But again, she blocked me.

"You're right, Miss Goring. I'm not going to shoot you. Not here, that is."

She waved the gun and me and pointed to the door.

"Get going, Miss Goring. After you," she said sharply.

I walked to the door slowly and turned the doorknob, but as soon as I opened the door and tried to step into the corridor, Prudence grabbed my arm and wound hers around it in a way that the tiny gun was practically hidden from sight, even though I could feel it straight up against my side.

"One wrong move, one wrong shout, and I will blow you into kingdom come," she warned softly.

"Where are we going?" I asked through gritted teeth.

"You and I are going for a walk, Miss Goring. Into the gardens. And when we get there, I'm going to place this gun in your hand, point it at your pretty little head and blow it to bits."

"But why? What have I done to you?" I demanded, as we started going down the stairs.

"You got in my way, that's what you did! Playing detective, as if you know anything about anything," she replied angrily.

The hallway was completely empty, since everyone was in the dining room, including the staff. I wished someone would poke their head out of the dining room at the sound of our footsteps on the stairs, but nobody did. At one point, I opened my mouth to cry for help, but the gun dug into my side sharply, and I realised that Prudence wouldn't hesitate to shoot me even if it meant she would get caught.

She cared for nothing at this point. She had nothing to lose and everything to gain from my death, at least in her opinion.

"Why aren't you in there?" I hissed. "Why aren't you at dinner?"

"You're not the only one who can fake a headache," she retorted. "I had a feeling you were up to something. I thought you'd try and break into Lady Belling's room. Little did I know that Miss Know-it-all was planning to ransack *my* room."

She threw open the front door, and we walked out of the house. I didn't know why, but the sound of the door shutting behind us sounded like a death knell, and my knees buckled with fear for the first time since Prudence caught me in her bedroom.

"Straighten up and don't try any of your tricks," she snarled.

I knew nobody from the house would see us disappearing into the gardens, because all the curtains would be drawn by now. I was all alone with this madwoman, walking to my fate, whatever that would be.

She dragged me to the small pond beyond the herb garden. It was very close to the spot where the flowerpot had almost killed me. She let me go when we were at the very edge of the pond, and I knew she planned to kill me here and throw my body into the pond.

But I had no intention of dying at her convenience. I had to keep her talking until someone realised I wasn't in my room. Why, oh why did I tell Florence that I wasn't to be disturbed all night? At the very least, I should have kept Scottie by my side.

"So it was you all along? You killed Maria Bocelli, and you tried to kill me the other night," I said desperately, to distract her from her main goal, which was to end my life.

"Yes, it was all me," she said proudly.

"Why?" I asked bluntly. "What did you get out of it?"

"I did it for him," she whispered. "It was all for him."

"Him? Do you mean…Bingo?" I asked in disbelief.

"Not Bingo…I hate that name! Call him Benjamin, Lord Belling," she breathed, and I tried not to gag at the beatific expression on her face. She looked positively demented. Which she was, otherwise, she wouldn't have killed Maria in the first place.

"I don't get it. Did you think he was going to marry you just because you killed his fiancée?"

"I just wanted him to be happy, and I knew he wasn't happy with that trollop."

She began to wave the gun dangerously close to me, so I took one step away from the pond while still trying to keep her talking.

"Was that why you sent her those nasty, anonymous letters? That was pretty cowardly of you, don't you think? If you had something to say to her, you should have said it to her face."

Her face twisted with anger, and she began to pace up and down in front of the pond.

"Did she even know my name? Trust me, Miss Goring, even if I had signed my full name to the letters, Maria Bocelli wouldn't have recognised it. Because in her eyes, I was not a person worth recognising. She never once greeted me or said a kind word to me. I might have been a piece of furniture where she was concerned."

"And for that, you killed her?" I whispered.

"Oh no, Miss Goring. I killed her because she was trying to cheat my dear Lord Belling out of the lifetime of happiness that he deserved. I was in the room when he got the first letter, you know."

"The one he burnt?"

She nodded in response.

"He was utterly horrified when he read the truth about her, but for some reason, he refused to believe it. Called it just a poison pen letter. But I knew it was all true, and could have kissed the writer's hand in gratitude. They had performed a great service. If only Lord Belling was less blinkered about the woman he was about to marry."

"Was it you who hid the second letter from him?"

When she nodded again, I gave her a mocking smile.

"That was rather stupid of you, because by then, he did want to call off the wedding. If only you had left well alone, the engagement would have been called off by now. The second letter with evidence of her perfidy would have been proof enough for him."

Prudence's face twisted in rage, and I thought she was going to leap at me in anger.

"But how did you do it?" I asked hastily, only relaxing a bit when she stopped in her tracks. "The murder. How did you pull it off?"

CHAPTER 28

"It was quite simple, actually. I stole the footman's livery when I decided I'd had enough of that woman, and that she was never going to leave Lord Belling. From there, it was very easy to take the key to the potting shed, since I had the full run of Lady Belling's room. I knew where everything was kept since I was the one who had to fetch and carry it all. *She* never lifted a finger if she could help it.

"I stole the cyanide, and on the day of the party, I went to my room before the performance, claiming I had a headache. Then I changed into that ridiculous costume and went downstairs just in time. If I had been late by even two minutes, John footman would have started service at Lord Belling's table," she crowed.

"But why did you wear that ridiculous hat? Don't you know footmen never wear a hat at table service?"

"Well, how else was I supposed to hide all my hair?" she demanded angrily. "I thought I could pull it off since the room was going to be dark, and nobody could see my face."

"And then you fumbled the tray," I said mockingly, just to keep her talking.

Where was Jimmy? Where was my mother? Did nobody care for me?

"I didn't fumble it," she snarled. "I did it on purpose, because it gave me time to drop the poison in both glasses."

"But why?" I asked, wondering why she took so much trouble to complicate our case.

"Because I did not want Lord Belling to be accused of her murder. I saw Mr Bellamy giving her a glass, and then, Lord Belling did the same. And both the glasses looked identical. I didn't know which was which. If I added the cyanide only to Lord Belling's glass, he would have been arrested immediately."

"And yet, that still almost happened," I pointed out.

"Why do you think I dropped that titbit about the first letter? I wanted to prove that someone had hidden the second one from him. On purpose."

I gasped in surprise.

"You were trying to frame Lady Belling for murder! But why would you do that?"

"Because she deserves it," yelled Prudence. "I wanted to pay her back for every taunt and every bit of abuse she's ever hurled at me. She thinks I'm absolutely useless. Well, we will see who's useless now, when your body is discovered days later in the pond, with her gun in there with you. We'll see if she doesn't swing for double murder. I know they don't always hang aristocrats, but they will make an exception for this one because you're such a beautiful girl. They will never forgive the woman who kills the wonderful Miss Goring," she said with mock-sweetness, and it absolutely terrified me.

I began to babble out of fear, saying whatever I thought would keep her from shooting me.

"Why did you throw a flowerpot at me. That was very rude!"

"Oh, I'm sorry, miss! Did I hurt your tender feelings? You deserved it for snooping into matters that weren't your concern. Why did you have to speak to John footman and discover that someone had stolen his livery? Could you not have left well alone?"

"I'm sorry, but I was just doing my job. You know you can walk away from this even now, Prudence. I can't stop you, since you're the one with the gun, after all."

"I think not, Miss Goring. After all, I need to be here for my dear Lord Belling. When he's crippled with grief over losing his mother to the hangman's noose, dear, frumpy Prudence will be on hand to console him and show him that he's never going to be alone," she said gleefully.

"Oh, dear Lord! That sounds even worse than being married to Maria," cried Bingo from somewhere behind us, and I could have wept with joy.

"Don't come near us, or I'll kill her," shrieked Prudence, whirling around in anger.

"I think not," said PC Peddle calmly, as he emerged from behind the cover of the house, a pistol trained on Prudence.

"Yeah, we won't let you. Dashed cheek, I say!"

That was Jimmy, who peeked around the side of the house, and when he saw that Peddle had a clear shot at Prudence, he came out with a rifle in his hand, followed by Bingo, with the matching one in his.

They were the real Tweedle Dee and Tweedle Dum, not the two under-gardeners, I thought fondly. Not a brain cell between the two of them, but they had the warmest hearts. Here they were, waving around large hunting rifles when they could barely shoot straight. I dearly hoped for all our sakes that the rifles were unloaded.

"Nooooo," shrieked Prudence furiously.

"Thank you all for coming to my rescue," I said gleefully. "I was really worried you wouldn't notice we were gone."

"Thank Peddle," said Jimmy.

"How did you know where to find me, Peddle?" I asked in surprise.

"I was watching the house, miss, when I saw Miss Sharp dragging you into the garden. I tapped on the dining room window to alert the family, and hightailed it here, and I was just in time to hear Miss Sharp's full confession. Put that gun down, miss. We have you covered from all sides," he said gently.

"No," said Prudence, simply. "I won't be arrested. I won't let all of you make a mockery of my love."

"Blimey! She's really mad," whispered Bingo.

Prudence threw her gun to the side, and before I could stop her, she jumped into the pond. I screamed in horror until I realised that she was actually quite a strong swimmer, despite her dress weighing her down.

I turned to Peddle worriedly.

"Aren't you going after her? She might escape."

"No chance of that, miss. The butler has already called the Yard, and some of our men are waiting on the other side of the pond. Look, they've got her," he said, pointing to the far shore.

Two burly policemen had dragged Prudence out of the water, kicking and screaming, and dragged her off to their car in handcuffs.

A police car screeched into the gravel path, ruining it forever, and DCI Burton leapt out of it while the motor was still running. He marched over to me and began yelling at me without giving me the chance to even open my mouth.

"How dare you risk your neck, you little fool? When I expressly told you not to confront her?"

"But I didn't confront her. She confronted me," I cried indignantly.

"And where did she do that?" he asked, fuming.

"Erm…" I realised that I should have kept my mouth shut. "In her room."

"And what were you doing in her room when I expressly told you not to confront her?"

And we were back to the same question. Well, I wasn't going to take this quietly.

"You don't own me, Henry Burton," I yelled back. "I am free to do whatever I want, even if it means confronting a madwoman. And this is the thanks I get for solving yet another murder for you!"

"That's it! You're not doing any more detective work, Miss Goring. You have officially retired," he snarled. "If I see you anywhere near another murder, I'm taking you straight to jail."

"Huzzah! Finally, a man of sense around here," cried my mother as she came around the corner of the house. "You must come to dinner, Detective Chief Inspector. And I'll make sure Kitty doesn't fake a headache that day."

"You're still not forgiven, Katherine Goring," said Lady Belling sternly. "But you may kiss my cheek."

I did as she asked, feeling as if I were approaching a vicious snake that was about to strike. But just as I was moving away, she patted my cheek and whispered, "Thank you for saving my Benjamin from the hangman's noose."

I grinned at her.

"To be honest, Lady Belling, you were in much more danger of being arrested for murder than Bingo ever was," I admitted sheepishly.

"Pfft! I'd like to see anyone try," she said grandly, and we both laughed as we walked back into the house.

EPILOGUE

The inquest was held two days later, and we all gave evidence against Prudence. Her fingerprints were found on the big bottle of cyanide retrieved from the shed, and on the remnants of the flowerpot she had thrown at me.

She refused to say a word, but there was enough evidence for the coroner to direct the police to file charges against Prudence in court so that she could be tried for murder. I knew she wasn't going to be hanged. No jury was going to find her remotely sane, so she would probably spend the rest of her life in an institution.

As for us, we moved back home, which was a relief, since Mother had taken an irrational dislike to Basil Perkins ever since Henrietta informed her that they were planning to be married soon.

Bingo had sworn off love for at least a year, although I wasn't sure how long that resolve would last. Meanwhile, the Cursed Ring was safely stored in a bank vault, where it would no longer cast its shadow of misfortune on unsuspecting victims.

Lady Belling wanted to press charges against Roberta

King for sending Bingo those awful letters, but we convinced her that it was a futile exercise.

Bingo returned Sidney's letter to him and invited him to attend Maria's funeral, which was a grand affair with almost all of London showing up to pay their respects to the beautiful woman who was killed at her own engagement party.

The salacious details of the case made it to the press almost immediately, but The Whispering Quill was suspiciously silent. Whether it was out of respect for Maria's death or for some other reason would remain to be seen.

As for me, I was still trying to convince my mother to allow me to set up a detective agency. And I was still trying to train Scottie to be my sidekick, but sometimes, I did wonder if he'd ever do anything more useful than chasing a ball.

"You're being too hard on him," said DCI Burton. "If it hadn't been for his obsession with balls, you would never have discovered the truth about Prudence Sharp."

He was a frequent dinner guest at Merivale Manor these days, especially since he soundly opposed my idea of becoming a lady detective.

One morning, I was reading a detective novel lent to me by Police Sergeant Peddle, who had earned his well-deserved promotion after all, when my mother burst into the parlour, waving a letter.

"Kitty, we've just been invited to Penelope Ponsonby's house party at Christmas," she cried joyfully.

~

*To know what happens at Penelope Ponsonby's house party, read **The Twelve Lies Of Christmas**, a Christmas murder mystery by Ella Strike!*

Read the following blurb to know more:

December 1923, London

Kitty Goring isn't in the mood for tinsel or trifle. But when her mother insists she attend Lady Penelope Ponsonby's legendary Christmas masquerade at Frostbrook House, Kitty dons her peacock mask, her emerald velvet gown, and prepares for a night of brittle small talk and bottomless champagne.

What she didn't prepare for was murder.

As snow drifts settle over the grand estate and champagne glasses clink beneath chandeliers, Lady Penelope unveils a scandalous parlour game: The Twelve Lies of Christmas.

But when one guest is found dead beside the punch bowl, the game turns deadly. And the lies begin to snowball. Trapped in a house full of high society's most cunning socialites, rivals, and a few too many "coincidental" strangers, Kitty must race to uncover which lie was worth killing for...before the killer strikes again. With her loyal Scottie dog by her side, an increasingly irate Detective Inspector Henry Burton underfoot, and mistletoe concealing more secrets than kisses, Kitty must solve the case before the twelve lies turn into twelve corpses.

The Twelve Lies Of Christmas *is the delightful fourth book in the* ***Kitty Goring Investigates*** *historical cozy mystery series.*

ABOUT THE AUTHOR

Ella Strike, author of historical cozy mysteries and chief sleuth of The Cozy Crime Club, lives in London.

When she's not penning murder mysteries or drinking copious amounts of Earl Grey, you can find her with her nose buried in a book or listening to true crime podcasts as she cooks.

Her stories are a mix of history, a dash of intrigue, and a whole lot of cozy, old-world charm.

She loves to hear from her readers, so feel free to write to her or follow her on Instagram.

If you enjoyed this book, do subscribe to The Cozy Crime Chronicles for your monthly dose of mystery, intrigue, cozy village life and roaring Twenties fun!

ALSO BY ELLA STRIKE

Murder At Merivale Manor

Sapphires And Secrets

The Twelve Lies Of Christmas

Made in the USA
Columbia, SC
08 July 2025

60517928R00100